The Korean Saviour

The Korean Saviour

Chandra Kant Jaisansaria

DAMICK PUBLICATIONS

Damick
PUBLICATIONS

DAMICK PUBLICATIONS

Website: www.damickpublications.com
Email: damickpublications@gmail.com
Contact: +91-9999212301

First Published by Damick Publications 2023

ISBN: 978-81-960820-6-2

Disclaimer

This is a work of fiction. Names, characters, businesses, places, events, locales, and incidents are either the products of the author's imagination or used in a fictitious manner. Any resemblance to actual persons, living or dead, or actual events is purely coincidental.

Neither the publisher nor the writer intends to outrage, insult, wound or hurt any religion or the religious sentiments, beliefs or feelings of any person(s) or class or community.

ॐ नमः शिवाय

Om Namah Shivaya

Acknowledgements

Writing this book has been a journey for me. The journey that I completed with the characters of this book and a few important people who worked as constant support to me. Here is my heartfelt gratitude to the people who helped me in shaping this book.

Readers, the ones for whom I tried my hands on fantasy for the first time. Believe me, your constant reminders have been pushing me ahead in completing this book in the best way possible.

Damini Aggarwal, my partner in crime. She has been reading every chapter despite not being interested in fantasy. The more I wrote, the more she got engrossed in the story. When we reached the last chapter, she said "This book would make an amazing bestseller".

Hatel Manilal Makani, my favourite reader, and a K-drama fan suggested me to watch the Korean series. I got inspired to write this book after watching the famous Korean series 'Guardian: The Lonely and Great God'.

Anchal Agarwal, the brilliant map maker of this book, worked and re-worked my ideas and came up with simple, elegant, and amazing maps that clearly showcase the real and fictional places this story is based on.

Mousumi Kalita Sachdeva, my friend and editor whose approval, suggestions, and corrections remain at the utmost priority before I publish any of my books. Despite being busy with her personal and official tasks, she worked on my book as if it was hers.

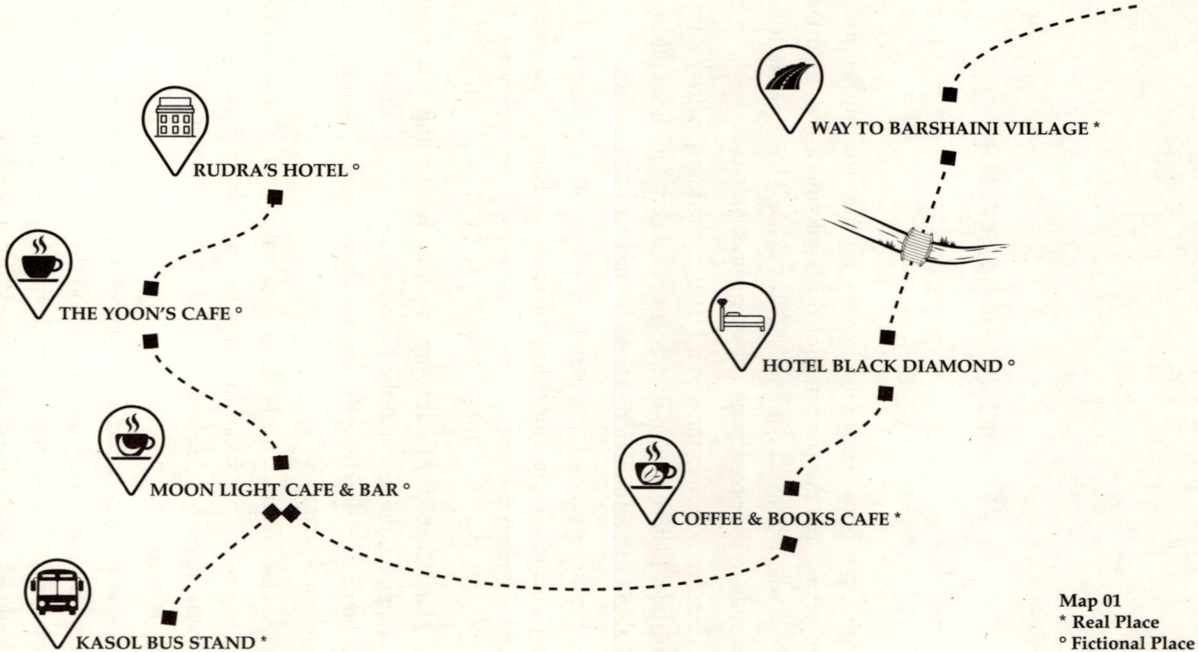
RUDRA'S HOTEL °
THE YOON'S CAFE °
MOON LIGHT CAFE & BAR °
KASOL BUS STAND *
WAY TO BARSHAINI VILLAGE *
HOTEL BLACK DIAMOND °
COFFEE & BOOKS CAFE *
Map 01
* Real Place
° Fictional Place

One

23 September 2019, 18:55 IST (Moon Light Café & Bar, Kasol)

"To the true love."

"To the true love." The couple wished and gulped their 13th peg of red wine. Unlike others this couple was special. Rudra, an Indian boy, and Kim Seo Yoon, a South Korean girl were truly and madly in love with each other.

Rudra was a rich brat with nothing to lose. He looked smart with his long curly hair that suited perfectly to his short-trimmed beard. His habit of always being neatly dressed made him look more appealing. The thing that Seo Yoon liked about Rudra was his eyes. Despite carrying a manly body, his eyes were notorious and curious like that of a child. Seo Yoon once said that Rudra's eyes carry a shine that made her fall for him.

Even Seo Yoon was different in her own way. She had a fair complexioned face, pitch-black long hair, and tiny cute eyes like other Korean girls, but the special thing about her was her bubbly nature. She still behaved like a kid that had plenty of things to learn and ample dreams to fulfill.

Visiting a café like this was routine for them. After each tiring day, they considered their evenings were meant to enjoy.

"Hey! Rudra. Hey! Yoon." A girl who was a regular visitor to the café greeted the couple while moving towards the dance floor.

"Hi! Tanya," The couple replied lowering their voice as they saw Tanya moving away from them.

"Guys, I guess this is enough for the day. You should go home now." The bartender suggested the couple.

"Oh! Common Daniel, we are just celebrating our togetherness. It's not even dark yet," Rudra replied.

"Yeah! I know that, but you have had more than your regular dose of wine today. And..."

"Shhh..." The bartender was about to complete when Seo Yoon asked him to keep quiet.

The bartender gave an ignoring look and moved with a tray of Israeli beer canes to the customers waiting at the table.

"Don't you think sometimes he pretends to be too caring?" Seo Yoon looked at Rudra and expected him to reply.

Rudra shrugged and moved his eyes around the café. It was his usual behaviour. He often replied with his expressions rather than words.

"You know what? You should learn to choose words and limit the expressions." The short-tempered Seo Yoon frowned at his behaviour.

"Yeah! But I don't think Daniel is an important person to speak about." Rudra replied giving an impish look.

"Great. So, before we start our daily melodrama fight, I should take my leave." Seo Yoon responded furiously getting frustrated by Rudra's cold replies.

"Sure. Have a good night then." Rudra replied in no mood to start the fight in public.

Seo Yoon grabbed her tote bag, kept some money on the table for bartender Daniel to take, and moved out of the Café without even looking at Rudra.

Rudra glued his eyes on the main door of the café and smiled. He has been mischievous and a little careless about Seo Yoon. This is because they have had ample fights every evening and the next day, they were together like 'nothing happened yesterday'.

The Moon Light Café's bartender Daniel had become more than a friend to the couple as they were daily visitors to his table. Being a friend, he always cared about them and prevented them from making a scene in public.

"She left already," Daniel asked Rudra taking the money that was kept on the table.

"Looks like…" Rudra ignored the question and took another peg of wine.

"One beer please…" A girl in her mid-twenties settled on the chair next to Rudra's.

"Sure" Daniel moved towards the freezer in order to fetch the beer.

Rudra looked at the girl and wondered where she was from. She wore a royal blue coloured deep neck top paired with some strange locket around her neck. Her red lipstick complimented the fair complexion of her face. Her dark brown hair ran from her head to her neck and touched her thighs. She looked as if she belonged to a royal family from the historical kingdoms. The only difference was she was in the attire that was from the present.

Rudra was about to move his eyes toward his wine glass when the girl uttered "Wondering where I have come from, stranger?"

Rudra couldn't react and his mouth went wide open. "Um… Uh… I Uh…"

"It's okay stranger. Say cheers to your companion today." She raised her beer cane and Rudra raised his wine glass to touch hers.

"Well. I have come from Kangra." The girl said looking into Rudra's eyes.

"How do you know what I was thinking? I mean, do you read minds?" Rudra asked getting surprised.

"Not exactly, but my guesses are almost always bang on." The girl chuckled.

"Seriously. You scared the shit out of me." Rudra tried to be friendly.

"I will someday." The girl looked into his eyes and said in a serious tone.

Rudra kept quiet and wondered about what should be his next line.

"Hey! Chill. I joke seriously sometimes." The girl laughed again and extended her hand toward Rudra "This is Disha and you?" she inquired.

"Well. I… I am Rudra." Rudra uttered with a handshake. "I am a localite here." He smiled thinking this is the end of the conversation.

"Ow. It's nice to meet you, Rudra." She replied extending her smile. "By the way, I am a lone wanderer. I often visit a lot of new and interesting places to explore nature." Disha continued her conversation.

"That's great. Even I settled here because of my love for travelling. I often visit a lot of hill stations on weekends and enjoy my weekdays here in the bar." Rudra uttered getting excited to meet a like-minded person.

"Wow. That's so cool Rudra. What's your next destination?" She was curious.

"We are planning a trip to Dalhousie and Khajjiar in the coming week." Rudra shared the information.

"Khajjiar, the mini-Switzerland of India," Disha confirmed.

"Of course. It is. Have you been to…?" Rudra inquired.

"Yes. Yes. Last month I have been to Dalhousie and Khajjiar. Believe me, man, it's really an amazing place to be at." She replied with a smile on her face.

"That's great. What's next then?" Rudra asked.

"Bus Stand." She replied.

"What?" Rudra tried to understand.

"The Bus Stand. Kasol Bus Stand. I have to leave for Kangra tonight." She looked at her wristwatch and wondered if she would find a bus leaving for Kangra.

"If you don't mind, may I accompany you to the bus stand?" Rudra asked getting excited to spend some more time with Disha.

"Sure. I won't mind that." She smiled.

Two

20:00 IST (Main Market Road, Kasol)

Rudra and Disha were walking on the road. The sky was filled with dense clouds, lightning and thunder, but it hardly mattered to the duo as it was a usual thing to happen at such hill stations.

"So, you said you settled here in Kasol because of your love for travelling. Originally, which place do you belong to?" Disha asked to start the conversation.

"I am basically from Delhi. I came to Kasol three years back and I chose to live here for a long while." Rudra replied.

"Um-Hmn, that's interesting," Disha uttered. "Have you ever been to Kangra?" She asked.

"Nope. I haven't." Rudra kept it short.

"You should. It's a wonderful place." She suggested.

"Sure. Very soon." Rudra smiled staring at her face.

"Uh... Maybe we have reached the bus stand." She directed her index finger towards the bus stand.

"Oh. Yes. We have." Rudra replied. "I didn't realize it because it was a very short walk." He looked at Disha and smiled.

"Sometimes, such short walks can give you the best of your memories." She smiled back and settled on one of the seats kept near the ticket counter.

"Well, I agree," Rudra replied settling beside Disha and wondering if this was the end of their meeting.

"When does the last bus to Kangra leave from here?" She interrupted Rudra's thoughts.

"Last bus?" Rudra looked at Disha in surprise. "I guess somebody has misguided you. There is no direct bus from Kasol to Kangra." He informed.

"Oh. Common Rudra, don't try to crack a joke here. Tell me…" She asked again.

"I am serious. I thought someone is going to pick you up from here, so I accompanied you. It is an overnight journey from here to Kangra and there are no direct buses to this route." Rudra replied.

"Shit." She uttered getting worried. "So that means I am stuck here for tonight." She looked at Rudra and confirmed.

"Well. You will have to stay in a hotel room tonight and you can leave at the dawn. I will get you a cab in the morning." Rudra suggested feeling a little joyous as their meeting just got extended.

"Hmm. What else can I do?" She stood up and took a deep breath. "Can you help me find a good hotel because the one that I checked out in the morning is literally not worth another night's stay?" She asked for a favour.

"That's not a problem. One of my friends owns a hotel which is just 2 kilometres away from here. Let's get you settled there for tonight." Rudra stood up, and they were about to leave when all of a sudden, the clouds started showering. "Well, looks like we'll have to wait here a little longer." Rudra looked at Disha and grinned.

"But why? We can walk in the rain and reach the hotel." Disha peeped out of the overhead shed willingly to get drenched.

Rudra held her hand and pulled her back. "Don't be a kid. I am sure you don't want to wake up with a high fever in the morning." Rudra said not realising that Disha had slipped her leg and fallen into his arms already. "Uh. I uh. I am so sorry… I just wanted to prevent you from getting wet. You might catch a cold due to this heavy rain." He continued feeling embarrassed and helped Disha get back on her feet.

Disha smiled and kept looking into Rudra's eyes. She wondered what Rudra was thinking at that particular point in time. Rudra on the other hand was feeling a little nervous and he wondered if he had committed a mistake. Subconsciously, he liked the way Disha was in his arms but apparently, he had to show that it was not at all his fault. "I think we should sit down until it stops raining," Rudra said breaking the silence.

Disha sat on the seat and looked at the rain. After a moment of silence, she said "I often wish to get drenched in the rain. To feel the cold breeze and the warmth of…" she paused.

"And the warmth of someone who can complete you." Rudra completed the sentence.

"Amazing," Disha said getting impressed with Rudra's fill-in-the-blanks. "You know what? I feel like you are my type." She continued and again paused.

"I didn't get you," Rudra said.

"The way you checked me out in the Café was something that a gentleman would never do." Disha kept her hand on Rudra's thigh.

"I…" Rudra was about to speak when Disha interrupted "Shh… I know you like alcohol, night outs, and…" she paused to play with Rudra getting a little close to him.

"And…?" Rudra wanted her to continue.

"And No Strings Attached." She smiled and looked straight into his eyes. They were full of lust and she wanted that lust to melt her down in the thinnest form of vapour. She did not move her hand any further as she wanted him to fill in the blanks.

Rudra sat still and dived deep into her eyes. He knew what she demanded and the adrenaline rush in his body hit him so hard that he couldn't do anything except whisper a few words in her eardrums "Let us fulfil each other's desire tonight".

Listening to this her smile widened. She stood up and signalled Rudra to show her the way to the hotel.

Three

24 September 2019, 08:00 IST (Room 33, Hotel Black Diamond, Kasol)

'Ting Tong' the bell rang and it was all silence inside the room. Rudra's eyelids struggled hard to open but failed. He was deep into his sleep. 'Tinggg… Tongg' the bell rang again and someone knocked on the door multiple times. "Heyaa! Michin Gae (Hey! Crazy Dog) wake up already, will you?" A man in his thirties stood outside the room and shouted in the Korean language.

Rudra fought hard with his sleep and finally managed to wake up. While getting up from the bed he realized that Disha was not there in the room. Not giving much importance to her whereabouts, he quickly moved towards the door and left it wide open.

"How many times do I need to tell you to sleep at your own hotel, not here?" The man at the door shouted and ran inside the room to clean it up for his guests.

Rudra barely landed his ears to the man and hurried up towards the exit of the hotel. This man, Jo Eun Sup was in his early thirties. He originally hailed from The Republic of Korea but settled in India for his livelihood. The only bond between him and Rudra was friendship. In fact, Rudra was lucky to have him in his life as Korean people are the best at keeping secrets.

While moving out of the hotel, Rudra tried to recollect the memories from the last night. All he could remember was entering the hotel room with Disha, but he couldn't recall whatever happened after that. In order to keep his last night a secret, he decided not to think much about it and move on.

08:15 IST (Moon Light Café & Bar, Kasol)

"Daniel. Have you seen Rudra? Do you know where he is?" Seo Yoon asked Daniel moving towards the bar counter.

"Nope. What happened?" Daniel asked getting curious.

"I don't know. His cell phone is switched off since yesternight and he is not at his hotel." Seo Yoon informed getting a little panicked.

"Don't worry Seo Yoon, you know he won't go anywhere out of Kasol without informing you. He must be at Eun Sup's." Daniel tried to calm her down.

"Yes, you're right. I must check at the Hotel Black Diamond." Seo Yoon left the bar and tried to reach Rudra's cell phone once again.

08:21 IST (Coffee & Books Café, Main Market, Kasol)

Rudra entered the roadside café and ordered his favourite coffee. While settling on the stool kept in front of the glass wall, he flipped the mobile phone out of his pocket. "Shit, it's dead." He uttered and plugged it in for charging.

"Did Disha leave the hotel before I woke up? Or she left the room in the night? Is she on her way to Kangra? Should I try to find her out and talk to her?" Several questions juggled in Rudra's mind but all he had to do was to try not to think much about it.

To divert his thoughts, he looked at the road which was visible through the glass wall. An old lady walked with her grandkids to the vegetable market. One of the kids carried her bag and the other one carried an umbrella for her. Rudra smiled and wondered what his grandmother would look like if she was alive today.

While noticing other people on the road, he saw Seo Yoon walking towards the Hotel Black Diamond. At once he wanted to move out and talk to her, but then he realized he will have to answer a lot of questions if he stops her. He also knew that Jo Eun Sup won't tell her anything about the last night so he relaxed sipping his coffee and deciding not to see her.

When he thought a little more about Jo Eun Sup, he remembered some of his friends from Delhi were supposed to visit him today at 09:00 IST. Hurriedly, he unplugged his half-charged mobile phone and switched it on. Ignoring all the missed call alerts, he dialled Jo Eun Sup's mobile number.

"Yeoboseyo (Hello!)" Eun Sup picked up the call.

"Annyeonghaseyo (Hello!)" Rudra replied trying to be friendly with Eun Sup fearing he would be scolded for his behaviour in the morning.

"Heyaa! Prick. You know I love it when you speak in Korean. You always get your things done from me with this little bribe of yours." Eun Sup shouted at Rudra as expected.

"Joesonghabnida (I'm Sorry)" Rudra replied anticipating that Eun Sup will calm down with his Korean apology.

"It's fine. Tell me what you want from me now." Eun Sup inquired melting on Rudra's Indo-Korean accent of speech.

"My friends from Delhi are visiting us today. We will have to take them to the Kheerganga Trek. Just leave the hotel now and meet me in five at Coffee & Books Café." Rudra ordered.

"Shit. Why can't you inform me a little earlier? I will have to rush now." Eun Sup replied and disconnected the call.

Four

09:01 IST (Hotel Black Diamond, Kasol)

"Annyeonghaseyo (Hello!)" Seo Yoon greeted the receptionist as she entered the hotel.

"Annyeonghaseyo Seo Yoonaa (Hello! Seo Yoon)" The receptionist replied with a smile on her face.

"I have something to ask you and I request you to keep it between you and me." Seo Yoon said standing at the front desk.

"Seo Yoonaa, it's been years we know each other. I am like your elder sister. You can count on me for that." The receptionist replied keeping her smile intact.

"I couldn't reach Rudra since yesternight. Daniel suggested me to check on him in your hotel. I mean, he mostly doesn't go to his hotel when he is too drunk." Seo Yoon spoke with a worried face.

"I was not on night duty. Sajangnim (Boss) was." The receptionist informed.

"Oh!" Seo Yoon replied getting more tense. She knew Jo Eun Sup won't tell her anything about the last night as he always cooks up something to save Rudra.

"Seo Yoona, Gwaenchanayo? (Seo Yoon, are you alright?)" The receptionist asked.

"Nan Gwaenchana (I am fine), will you please get me a cup of coffee? I am feeling a bit stressed." Seo Yoon requested.

"Sure, I will." The receptionist stood up and moved towards the pantry.

While the receptionist was busy heating the coffee vending machine, Seo Yoon quickly jumped towards the computer kept at the reception and started looking for last night's CCTV footage of the camera which was hung above the main door of the hotel.

23/09/2019 22:12 IST

Rudra entered the hotel keeping his left hand on a girl's waist. Though the camera only showed the girl's back, her figure could tell that she was in her mid-twenties. They both moved towards the reception on their right-hand side. After a brief discussion with Rudra, Jo Eun Sup handed over a key to him. Rudra thanked Jo Eun Sup, smiled at the girl, and escorted her to the left-hand side lobby.

Seo Yoon understood the fact that Rudra had been to any of the rooms on the left side lobby of the hotel. She tried to zoom in on the CCTV footage where Eun Sup was handing over the key to Rudra. Despite trying hard, she couldn't read the room number scribbled on the key.

A drop of tear poured on the computer keyboard when Seo Yoon came to know that Rudra did not come out of the room even after four hours of his entry. She wished her so-called true love to be actually true, but this act of Rudra made her realize that true love was not in her fate.

She went ahead and decided to check the remaining footage.

24/09/2019 02:47 IST

Jo Eun Sup yawned and got up from his chair. He moved towards the main door of the hotel and locked it from the inside. Then he turned towards the right-side lobby and went to his room to get some sleep, but he left the lights of the hotel entrance switched on for security purposes.

24/09/2019 03:00 IST

The lights of the left side lobby flickered and went off. The right-side lobby went dark too. It looked like the lights of the main entrance and the reception played on and off with each other for a short span of time and they all went off at the end.

Seo Yoon went a little closer to the computer screen to analyze what was happening.

All the lights suddenly turned on and someone moved from the left lobby towards the front of the main entrance. It was the same girl who went inside the room with Rudra.

Seo Yoon went cautious and kept looking at the screen.

The girl turned her head up and looked at the CCTV camera that was hung above the main door. She smirked and a frame of black smoke surrounded her. She kept looking into the camera and vanished within a fraction of a second.

Seo Yoon jumped on her seat, getting afraid of what she just saw. Her face turned red and her eyes went wide open. She did not know what to do. Suddenly, a hand appeared on her right shoulder; she moved her eyes towards the right but couldn't gather the strength to check who it was. She was about to shout aloud, but someone uttered something from behind…

"Seo Yoonaa, It's me." The receptionist said moving in front of Seo Yoon.

Seo Yoon looked at her, cried, and jumped to hug her.

"I saw the footage, Seo Yoonaa. I was standing just behind you and watching everything. I think the girl in the camera was an evil spirit." The receptionist said keeping the coffee cup on the table.

Seo Yoon listened to her but did not react. She was completely frozen out of fear.

The receptionist took out Seo Yoon's mobile phone from her pocket and transferred the entire CCTC footage file to it. "You must hurry up and show it to Sajangnim (Boss). He belongs to the family of shamans. Maybe he knows how to deal with such spirits. He will surely help you." The receptionist suggested Seo Yoon show the footage to Jo Eun Sup.

"Ne, Kamsahamnida. (Yes, Thank You.)" Seo Yoon took her mobile phone back, bowed, and left the hotel in a hurry.

"Be careful Seo Yoonaaa..." The receptionist shouted from behind while Seo Yoon slowly went out of her eyesight.

Five

09:32 IST (Kasol Bus Stand)

It was a bright morning with no rainy clouds in the sky. Rudra and Jo Eun Sup were waiting for Rudra's friends at the bus stand. They both stood under the same overhead shed where Rudra and Disha had spent a few hours of their last night.

Rudra was lost in his thoughts. Meeting a stranger like this was not new to him, but this one was different. What pinched him the most was that he did not remember anything that happened after he entered the hotel room with Disha.

Jo Eun Sup's eyes were stuck on the road that led the buses from other cities to Kasol. Looking at the time on his mobile phone, he wondered if the bus was running late. His phone vibrated, and he looked at Rudra, who was still wondering about Disha's whereabouts.

"Heyaaa. It's Kim Seo Yoon calling." Jo Eun Sup raised his mobile screen in front of Rudra's eyes and shouted.

"Muhyo (What?) cut the call. Don't answer it." Rudra snatched the phone and disconnected the call.

"Wae (Why?) What's wrong with you guys?" Jo Eun Sup took his mobile phone back and dialled Seo Yoon's number.

"It's nothing. I just need a break. Please..." Rudra folded his hands and requested Eun Sup not to call her back.

Jo Eun Sup disconnected the call and flipped the mobile phone back into his pocket. "Fine. Do whatever you want." He uttered looking towards a luxury bus that just arrived at the station.

"Here they are," Rudra said and moved towards the bus.

"Hello! Rudra." Rudra's six feet tall bodybuilder friend Dhruv greeted in his heavy voice while getting off the bus.

"Hey man! How have you been?" Rudra took a step forward and shook his hand with him.

"Amazing as always." Dhruv smiled flaunting a big tattoo of Lord Shiva that was scribbled on his left arm.

"Ooh, Wa. (Wow.)" Joe Eun Sup looked at his tattoo and exclaimed.

"How about you stop showing off your tattoo big man?" A fair-complexioned slim girl in a white tank top and skin-fitted black jeans got off the bus and questioned Dhruv. "Rudra, you can just ignore this guy." She looked at Rudra and winked.

"Ah! Don't worry Shivi, I don't give much importance to him." Rudra smiled and realized these people haven't changed a bit in the last few years.

"I'm sorry guys, I forgot to introduce, this is..."

"Jo Eun Sup." Both of them said in a chorus before Rudra could complete.

"Hey! Buddy. I'm Dhruv."

"Hi! Eun Sup. This is Shivi." They both shook hands with Jo Eun Sup one by one.

"Hello! Guys. It is nice to meet you. But how do you know me?" Jo Eun Sup inquired.

"This asshole talks about only two people from Kasol. Kim Seo Yoon and Jo Eun Sup." Dhruv said while they all moved towards the exit of the bus stand.

"Oh. I see." Jo Eun Sup replied wondering what else he should say.

"So, what's the plan?" Shivi looked at Rudra and asked.

"Well, you guys can freshen up and take breakfast at my hotel, and then we will go to Barshaini Village from where the trekking to Kheerganga starts," Rudra replied waving at a taxi to stop.

"Hmm. That sounds like a plan." Shivi said nodding her head and they all boarded the taxi towards Rudra's hotel.

09:34 IST (Kasol Main Market)

"Darn, Eun Sup is not picking up the calls. I must hurry to my room and take help from my uncle." Seo Yoon got too much worried and ran towards her café 'The Yoon's Café'.

"Annyeong (Hello!)" the receptionist greeted when Seo Yoon entered the café, but Seo Yoon did not respond and quickly took the stairs to the first floor. Hurriedly getting into her room, she locked the door from inside and moved towards a huge painting that was hung on a wall.

This painting looked as if it was of a warrior. The man in the painting wore armour and held a sword in his right hand. His long hair was untied and his eyes reflected his confidence to win over the enemies. Park Jeong Su, his name was scribbled below the painting.

Soe Yoon took out a special perfume from her almirah and poured a drop of it on the painting. A blue flame appeared all over the painting and it shined. It shined so bright that Seo Yoon couldn't keep her eyes open. Slowly the bright light started dimming and a shadow emerged in front of the painting.

"Seo Yoonaa" The shadow uttered.

"Samchon. (Uncle.)" Seo Yoon opened her eyes and moved toward the shadow that turned into a man who resembled the warrior in the painting.

The man who appeared in front of Seo Yoon was neither a human nor a ghost, he was Park Jeong Su, a lonely and great god on the planet. In other words, he was a goblin. He had the power to travel through time and space and that is how he travelled from South Korea to The Yoon's Café in a fraction of a second.

"Why did you summon me, Seo Yoona?" The goblin asked.

A drop of tear rushed out of Seo Yoon's left eye and she helplessly looked at the goblin.

"Gwaenchana? (Are you alright?)" The goblin asked another question.

"I need your help, Sumchon (Uncle). I think the love of my life is in danger." Seo Yoon said sobbing hard.

"You mean that irresponsible punk. Haisshhh…" The goblin uttered settling on a chair. "I told you not to settle in India because of that idiot. I knew he would land you in trouble someday and see…" He continued.

"I know uncle but I can't live without him. Please help me." Seo Yoon requested folding her hands in front of the goblin.

"Okay. Calm down. Tell me what happened." The goblin inquired.

Seo Yoon moved towards the goblin's chair and placed her mobile phone on the table laying in front of him. She played the footage that she took from the hotel. The goblin carefully watched the entire footage and the scene where Disha looked at the camera and vanished into black smoke. "It's the Bulack Soule." The goblin uttered.

"Muhyo, Bulack Soule? (What, a Black Soul?)" Seo Yoon confirmed.

"Yes. An evil spirit that gets pleasure in giving pain to others. Once it starts chasing someone, it doesn't finish without getting what it wants." The goblin informed.

Listening to this, the lines of fear appeared on Seo Yoon's forehead and she asked "But why is it behind Rudra? What does it want from him?"

"I don't know, but someone who captures such spirits can tell." The goblin said.

"Nugu? (Who?)" Seo Yoon looked at the goblin with curiosity.

"Jeosung Saja (A Grim Reaper)" The goblin reverted.

"The God of Death?" Seo Yoon confirmed keeping her eyes wide open.

"Eo (Yes)." The goblin replied.

"But we don't have grim reapers in India." Seo Yoon sat on a chair with her head down in dismay.

"Then we will have to bring the one we know from Korea." The goblin said.

"You mean Lee Ji Young?" Seo Yoon confirmed.

"Eo (Yes)." The goblin replied.

"But how?" She inquired.

"Just wait here. I will be right back." The goblin stood up from the chair and went back into the painting as he came.

Six

13:30 KST (Seoul, South Korea)

A tall, handsome man walked through the neat and clean roads of Seoul, the capital of South Korea. He wore a complete black outfit, making his whitish complexion look more adorable. The passing by young ladies stopped for a moment while he crossed his path with them.

They say death is always frightening, but this man was an irony to the personification of death. Even being a Grim Reaper, he looked so smart that any girl on that road would smilingly die to live with him.

Without paying much heed to the ladies out there, the grim reaper moved ahead and entered a garments shop. The only thing he found unique about the garments shop was a mannequin displayed at its entrance. This mannequin wore a pitch-black suit that attracted the grim reaper.

"Eoseoooseyo (Welcome)," The shopkeeper greeted putting a smile on his face.

"I want to buy this outfit; can I try it?" The grim reaper asked pointing at the black dress.

The shopkeeper looked at the young man and wondered 'Why would a man who is already in a black outfit demand another black dress?'

"Geogiyo? (Excuse me?)," The grim reaper broke the shopkeeper's chain of thoughts.

"Au, Joesonghamnida (Oh! I am sorry)." The shopkeeper bowed and apologised realising he had to attend to his customer's demand. He moved out of the sales counter and arranged the black dress for the young man's trial. "Here it is, Sir. The trial room is on your right. You can check the fitting." The shopkeeper pointed towards a trial room and smiled.

"Hmm" The grim reaper showed some attitude, took the suit, and moved towards the trial room.

When he entered the trial room, he saw a painting of a man who wore a black suit similar to the one he was about to try. "Huh. I will look much better than you." The grim reaper smirked looking at the man in the painting and locked the door from inside. He showed his back to the painting and adjusted himself in front of the mirror.

"Black is forever." He smiled and put the black shirt on. Adjusting the collar and buttoning the cuffs, he wore the jacket too. His smile went wide when he put the black round hat on his head. "Now no one can see me. I can even walk out of the shop without paying for the suit." He thought and unlocked the door.

"Shit." He uttered and put both his hands in front of his underwear realising that he forgot to put his pants on. He quickly ran inside the trial room and locked the door. Hurriedly, he slipped his legs one by one into the pant and was about to button the waist.

"Jeosung Saja (Grim Reaper), you need to come with me." The goblin appeared from the painting and put his hand on the grim reaper's shoulder.

The grim reaper quickly buttoned his waist and said "Naneun Jeoseung Saja Imnida (I am a grim reaper), you cannot take me anywhere without my permission."

"Jinjja (Really?)," The goblin asked keeping his right hand on the grim reaper's collar and dragged him into the painting.

10:30 IST (The Yoon's Café, Kasol)

The goblin and the grim reaper landed at Seo Yoon's room in Kasol.

"Heyaa! Dokkaebi. (Hey! Goblin.) You can't forcefully drag me to some other place like this." The grim reaper freed himself from the goblin's grip and shouted adjusting his collar.

"Here he is, Seo Yoonaa." The goblin directed his finger at the grim reaper who stood on his right.

Seo Yoon carefully looked around and found no one besides the goblin.

"Samchon (Uncle), there is no one beside you." Seo Yoon uttered thinking the goblin was in a mood to play pranks with her.

The grim reaper stood quiet carrying a mischievous smile on his face and raising his eyebrows.

"Hmm." The goblin shook his head upside down realising the secret behind the grim reaper's invisibility. He quickly patted the grim reaper's head and his black round hat fell on the ground.

"Taddaaa" The goblin uttered and smiled.

"Dangsineun (You...)" The grim reaper picked his hat from the ground and was about to say something when the goblin showed him his right hand and signalled him to keep quiet.

"Naega... (I...)" The grim reaper tried to speak again when the goblin again signalled him to keep quiet.

"Au (Oh). Here he is. How did I forget that the grim reapers become invisible when they wear a black hat?" A smile appeared on Seo Yoon's face when she finally saw the grim reaper, Lee Ji Young.

"Haaah… I have never seen someone so happy meeting a Grim Reaper." The grim reaper looked at Seo Yoon and smirked.

"What a poor joke." The goblin sniggered.

"If the Almighty wouldn't have given you the punishment to live forever. I swear, I would have kicked you to the afterlife." The grim reaper frowned at the goblin.

"Would you please stop fighting like kids?" Seo Yoon shouted at both of them begging their attention. "Rudra seems to be in serious trouble and I don't think I have plenty of time to witness your fight." She continued.

"What?" The grim reaper looked at Seo Yoon and questioned.

"Yeah. Uncle Park Jeong Su brought you here to help me out with this." Seo Yoon handed over her mobile phone to the grim reaper to let him watch the footage.

The grim reaper curiously saw the entire footage and uttered in surprise "The Bulack Soule?"

"Eo (Yes), The Bulack Soule." The goblin repeated. "Look, you are a grim reaper and you have the powers to see the past and present of any soul wandering on this earth. I'm sure you can tell us why it is behind Rudra." He continued looking into the grim reaper's eyes.

"But I don't think it is a good idea as you know we do not have permission to meddle with human lives." The grim reaper looked at the goblin and spoke.

"I know… and we aren't meddling with their lives. We just need to know why it is chasing Rudra and that is it." The goblin informed.

"Fine. Let me look through the eyes of the black soul once again." The grim reaper said settling on a chair and rewinding the footage.

Seven

11:15 IST (Main Market, Kasol)

After having their breakfast, Rudra and his friends walked towards the bus stop from where they could board the bus for Barshaini Village. Kasol's main market looked empty as it witnesses a smaller number of tourists in the month of September. But this made their trip more peaceful and worth enjoying. They all silently marched through Kasol Park and then through a small bridge enjoying the scenic beauty of the place.

"Damn! This place. I wish I had come here before." Shivi said noticing the river that flowed below the bridge.

"I knew you will regret not accepting my invitation to visit Kasol in the last three years." Rudra winked.

"It's just the beginning. The places you're about to visit are much more beautiful than you can ever imagine. You'll see once you reach there." Jo Eun Sup smiled.

"Oh, I so wish. By the way, Jo Eun Sup can I ask you something?" Shivi looked curious.

"Sure." Jo Eun Sup replied.

"This place, Kasol. It is known as Mini Israel. How on earth did you Korean guys settle here?" She looked at Jo Eun Sup and expected an answer.

"Well, I came here when I was twenty. I liked this place so much that I had this thought in my mind 'If Israeli people can live here, why can't I?' and then I started working in the Hotel Black Diamond until the owner died and I was handed over its keys as I was the sole caretaker of the hotel." Jo Eun Sup narrated his story in one go.

"Wow, that's pretty interesting," Shivi replied.

"Yeah. It is." Jo Eun Sup smiled.

"What's up with you big man? Why are you so quiet today?" She looked at Dhruv who was silently walking with them.

"I had an amazing breakfast today. I wish I could have three more dosas." Dhruv replied still imagining the extra-large masala dosas that were served to him during breakfast.

"Huh. Here we are talking about some interesting stuff and this guy is still feeling hungry." She laughed.

"Oye! You can't eat much when you have to trek. It will be troublesome for you." Rudra said looking at Dhruv.

"Yeah! That's why I ate so less today." Dhruv replied with a sad face.

'This guy is literally a tanker. He had six large dosas today and he is still feeling hungry. My goodness.' Jo Eun Sup thought but did not utter anything.

"Common on guys, we have to board this one," Rudra said quickly moving towards the white and green coloured bus that just arrived at the bus stop.

"Woohoo. I am excited about the trek." Shivi exclaimed moving inside the bus.

"Damn! You are." Rudra replied noticing Shivi's excitement.

They were all seated on the bus in a group of two. Rudra was sitting beside Jo Eun Sup in the front seat and Dhruv was sitting beside Shivi in the back seat. The bus started moving and zig-zagged on curvy roads that led to Barshaini.

Rudra took his mobile phone out to see how many calls did he miss from Seo Yoon.

"Rudra, you did wrong spending your last night with that stranger girl and now you are ignoring Seo Yoon's calls. It is not good." Jo Eun Sup said noticing the missed call list on Rudra's mobile phone.

"Eun Sup. I know I did the wrong thing. But trust me, I am trying to figure out how should I confront Seo Yoon after what I did last night. I never said I will not talk to her and confess everything. It's just that I want some time." Rudra said in a low voice so that no one else could hear their conversation.

"Okay. But don't be too late." Jo Eun Sup looked at Rudra and suggested.

"I won't be. And please, don't pick up her calls till we are back." Rudra requested Jo Eun Sup.

"Fine. I won't." Jo Eun Sup replied with no intention to ignore Seo Yoon.

"Guys! Look at these little lambs. Oh! My god. They are so cute. I wish I could play with one of these." Shivi sneaked out of the window and shouted looking at a group of lambs passing by their bus.

"Sit properly Kiddo. It's a single-lane road. You may lose your head to any vehicle coming from the other side." Dhruv pulled Shivi back onto the bus.

"Ughh… what's wrong with you today? You are not enjoying at all." Shivi blustered.

"Calm down, Shivi. Dhruv is right. Taking your head out of the bus in excitement is not good. We will send some of these lambs to your house in Delhi. You can make your Instagram reels with them." Rudra laughed and the others joined him.

Shivi too gave a fake smile and pinched Dhruv's biceps.

"Okay. Okay. Don't do it. I am sorry. I was just playing around." Dhruv apologized laughing when Shivi constantly pinched him at different parts of his body.

"Some kids never grow." Rudra smiled nodding his head from left to right.

Eight

11:30 IST (The Yoon's Café, Kasol)

The grim reaper kept the CCTV footage paused at a point where the black soul looked at the camera and smirked. He constantly looked into her eyes and did not speak anything. The goblin and Seo Yoon's curiosity rose multi-fold with the passage of every minute. After not hearing from him for the last fifteen minutes, the goblin gave up on his patience and patted the grim reaper's shoulders "Jeosung Saja (Grim Reaper)… Ya Jeosung Saja (Heya! Grim Reaper)."

"Mwo? (What?)" The grim reaper uttered.

"Are you lost in the black soul's eyes or what?" The goblin asked.

"Let me concentrate, will you?" The grim reaper said aloud.

"Sure, but we don't have hundreds of years to wait for your reply." The goblin reverted.

"Seo Yoona, will you please ask your uncle to keep quiet? Maybe bring him some coffee so that he can stay calm until I am finished." The grim reaper looked at Seo Yoon and spoke.

"Samchon (Uncle), you just sit down and let him concentrate. I will just be back with some coffee for both of you." Seo Yoon requested and walked towards the exit of the room.

As soon as Seo Yoon left the room, the grim reaper quickly moved towards the goblin and said "Heyaa! This bulack soule has something to do with Rudra's previous life and it is chasing him in this life as well, but we can't stop it at this moment."

"What? But why?" The goblin asked.

"I will tell you that in detail when the right time comes, but the important thing here to note is that two of Rudra's friends are in grave danger." The grim reaper informed.

"You mean the black soul is after Rudra's friends now?" The goblin confirmed.

"Eo (Yes), but we don't have to tell anything to Seo Yoon yet. If we do so, she will force us to meddle with human lives and help them. And we aren't supposed to do that." The grim reaper suggested.

"Okay. So, what do we do now?" The goblin inquired.

"Just wait for the right time. We will come to India again when we have our roles to play." The grim reaper said.

"Roles?" The goblin asked.

"Nothing. Just let things happen as they are meant to be and let's go back to Korea for a while." The grim reaper replied.

"Wait. Will Rudra be safe?" The goblin asked curiously.

"For the time being, yes. When I was looking into the future, I could not see any death card in Rudra's name." The grim reaper replied.

"And did you see his friend's names on the death cards?" The goblin fired another question.

"Even if I saw, we can't save them. Seo Yoon will be here any moment, so remember what I just said to you. Okay?" The grim reaper looked into the goblin's eyes and confirmed.

"Uff! It's going to be really challenging to convince Seo Yoon and tell her nothing is wrong." The goblin returned to the chair.

"The more challenging will be to face her if anything happens to Rudra's friends and when she will know that we lied." The grim reaper moved towards the goblin and kept Seo Yoon's mobile phone on the table.

"Hot coffee for you both." Seo Yoon entered the room and handed over the cups of coffee to the goblin and the grim reaper.

"Gomawo. (Thank You)." They both said in chorus and looked at each other feeling a little nervous.

"Wae geu-rae? (What's wrong?) Is Rudra in danger?" Seo Yoon looked at their worried faces and asked.

"Anniyo (No). He is safe." The grim reaper uttered signalling the goblin not to tell her anything as decided.

"Haashhh… Thank God." Seo Yoon took a sigh of relief. "But what about that Black Soul? Why was it after Rudra?" She asked looking into the goblin's eyes.

"It's just that she followed Rudra and later on she came to know that he was not the person she was looking for." The grim reaper again replied when the goblin was about to utter something.

"Oh! It's such a relief to hear that." Seo Yoon smiled and sat beside the goblin. "Samchon, Gwaenchanayo? (Uncle, are you alright?)" She asked the goblin who still looked worried.

"Ne (Yes). It's just that I am feeling a little tired. I think the problem is solved now and we should leave for Korea." The goblin stood up keeping the cup of coffee on the table.

"Samchon…"

Seo Yoon was about to say something when the goblin broke in and said "You take care of yourself and don't worry about Rudra. He will be back to you as he always does."

Listening to this Seo Yoon smiled and hugged the goblin. "Kamsahamnida (Thank You)." She said looking into the grim reaper's eyes who stood right beside the goblin.

"Anneyong (Good Bye), the goblin patted Seo Yoon's shoulder ignoring eye contact with her, and moved towards the painting.

"Stop! Take me with you." The grim reaper shouted from behind when the goblin was about to enter the painting.

"My cup." Seo Yoon uttered lowering her voice when she noticed her coffee cup in the grim reaper's hand.

"Here." The grim reaper handed over the cup and jumped towards the painting when the goblin had already half entered the painting.

They both disappeared, and Seo Yoon sat on the chair feeling a bit relaxed. She was worried about Rudra's life more than the fact that Rudra had spent his last night with a stranger. While checking her mobile phone, she noticed that she had received a text message from Jo Eun Sup. "Seo Yoonaa, Rudra is with me and we are on our way to the Kheerganga Trek with two of his friends from Delhi. He is fine but not in the right mood to talk. Don't worry. I will fix his mood and bring him to you as soon as we are back from the trek." It read.

"Thank You, Eun Sup. Please take care of that idiot." Seo Yoon replied and moved toward her bedroom to take a nap.

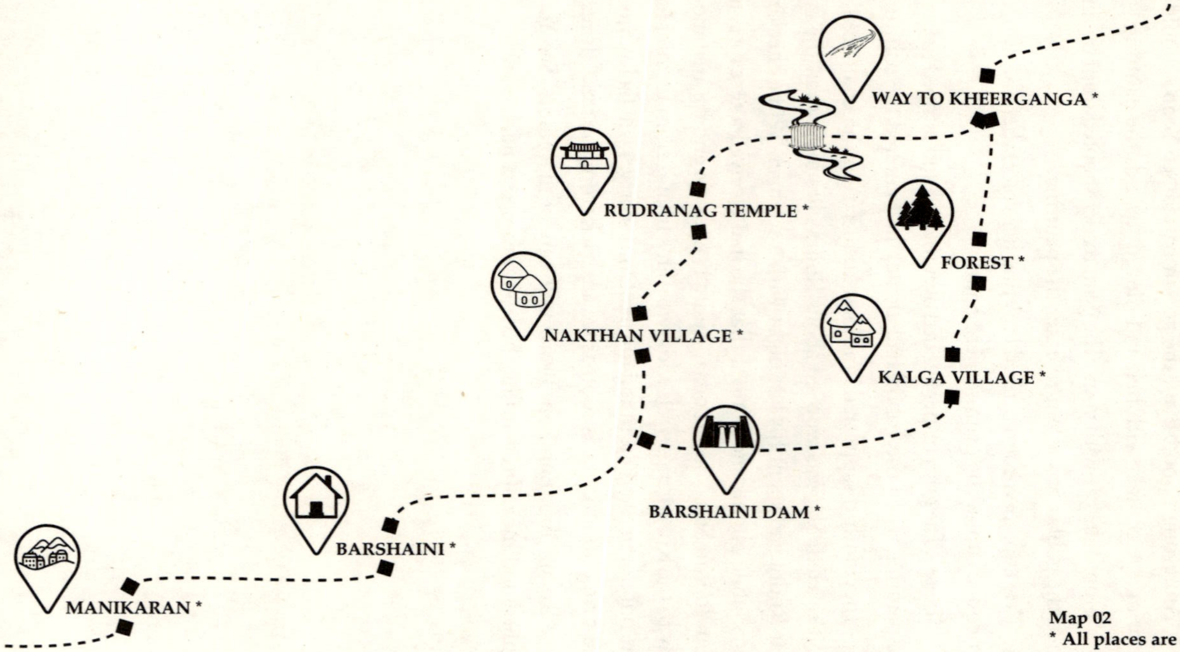

Map 02
*** All places are real**

Nine

11:46 IST (Manikaran)

"Traveling by bus between two hill stations is a completely different experience. Apart from being able to closely notice the culture and people, we also get to enjoy an adventurous ride on the steep and sloppy roads of the hills." Dhruv said to Shivi.

"True. At a moment these sharp turns take your breath away, but the next moment makes you realize that life is all about risks. Once you are through your risks, you get rewarded with beautiful days ahead." Shivi replied constantly gazing outside the window. "Hey! Rudra, what is this divine structure appearing on the left side of the road?" Shivi asked waking up Rudra who was taking a nap.

"Ah… This beautiful place is Manikaran. The divine structure that you are asking about is Manikaran Gurdwara." Rudra uttered waking up.

"Wow! Is this the place where people come to take a holy hot spring bath?" She confirmed.

"Yeah, how do you know that?" Rudra asked struggling to keep his eyes open.

"You know Mr. Rudra, I have a habit of researching the place I plan to visit," Shivi replied in a proud tone.

"Umm Hmm. So, tell me Ms. Shivi. What's special about this place?" Rudra asked.

"Well. It is said that taking a bath in the hot boiling sulphur spring here helps cure skin diseases." Shivi replied.

"That's interesting," Dhruv exclaimed removing his earplugs. "Are we getting down here to visit the Gurdwara?" He asked.

"Not right now." Jo Eun Sup replied. "We will pay a visit to this place while coming back from Kheerganga." He ensured.

"Why don't you take a nap, big man?" Shivi suggested Dhruv putting his earplugs back into his ears.

"Yeah. Instead of listening to your loud noise, I guess I should get some sleep." Dhruv replied closing his eyes and switching his playlist on.

"This tom and jerry fight is never-ending. I wonder how they find something to fight over every time." Rudra said to Jo Eun Sup.

"Hahaha. Still, they are good friends and they get along very well." Jo Eun Sup smiled. "I wonder if three of you are college friends." He questioned.

"Not exactly Eun Sup. Rudra and I are college friends and we met Dhruv at a startup fest in Delhi." Shivi answered.

"Oh! To be true, I am Rudra's friend for the last three years now, but he didn't tell me anything about his college days or you guys." Jo Eun Sup informed.

"Hmm. Quite expected. He is completely different from what he was during our college." Shivi replied.

'Himachal Road Transportation welcomes the onboarding passengers. The next station is Barshaini. We will reach our destination by 12:35 IST. We wish you have a comfortable journey with us.'

The announcement on the bus took over their conversation for a short while.

"Well, it looks like I have plenty of time to know how Rudra was during his college days." Jo Eun Sup continued the conversation.

"Yeah. Even I would like to relive those moments." Rudra said wanting to recollect the moments from his past.

"Okay." Shivi responded and started narrating the story "When Rudra joined the college, he was a very shy kind of a guy. He even hesitated to introduce himself properly, but when he noticed his classmates being very outspoken, he too started gelling well with the others. He did good at his studies and groomed himself over time. In fact, within few months he was the centre of attraction. He topped the class in a few subjects at the end of the semester and the girls who thought he was dumb went mad over him." Shivi looked at Rudra and saw him smiling over his praises. "I wondered how a monkey-faced guy could be so good at studies." She winked at Jo Eun Sup pulling Rudra's leg.

"Huh. Jealousy still prevails." Rudra uttered while the smile vanished from his face.

"Hey! I was just kidding." Shivi and Jo Eun Sup laughed noticing Rudra's facial expressions.

"But let me tell you one thing, he was so talented that he became my best friend and together we topped the class. All thanks to me." Shivi shrugged and gave another punch of laughter.

"This girl is seriously impossible." Rudra burst out of laughter and noticed Dhruv who still kept his eyes closed.

"Shall I?" Shivi asked Rudra if she should remove Dhruv's earplugs and involve him in their chit-chats.

"Nah. We will tell him later about what did he miss. Why should Dhruv have all the fun?" Rudra replied.

"Okay. But seriously Jo Eun Sup, Rudra was a favourite student to all the professors and he even got two proposals during college. In fact, one of the girls even kissed him on his cheek in front of the whole class." Shivi continued.

"Jinjja (Really?) Dangsin Chaegoya (You're the best)." Jo Eun Sup smilingly looked at Rudra keeping both his thumbs up.

"Well, he denied the proposal stating he already had a girlfriend," Shivi informed shattering Jo Eun Sup's excitement.

"What? Rudra, you didn't tell me you have one more girlfriend. Let me inform Seo Yoon about this." Jo Eun Sup said trying to look a bit serious.

"Oops," Shivi uttered teasing Rudra.

"Common now, tell him the truth." Rudra insisted.

"So the girl he loved broke up with him and he was sad about it for almost two years," Shivi replied.

"Ah. That breaks my heart." Jo Eun Sup mischievously uttered keeping his right hand on his heart.

"Breakups are not meant to be taken seriously, bro. I get a crush on every second girl I meet and they always break my heart." Dhruv said putting his earplugs aside.

"Damn! This man was listening to us throughout." Rudra wondered while all others laughed aloud.

'This is Barshaini Station. Stand clear of the doors. Please do not forget to take all your belongings. We hope you had a comfortable journey with us.' The announcement in the bus marked their arrival at the Barshaini bus stand from where they had to continue their journey on foot.

Ten

12:46 IST (Barshaini)

As they all silently moved from the Barshaini bus stand towards the beginning of the Kheerganga trek, the weather took a romantic turn from sunny hot to freezing cold. The sudden change of weather was nothing new in the month of September, but the way it changed within a few minutes was soul soothing. At least at the beginning of their excursion, one thing was sure and that was comfort, which wasn't foreseeable under the scorching heat that prevailed in the early hours of the day.

Looking at the sky, Rudra asked Jo Eun Sup if it was expected to rain that day, to which Jo Eun Sup replied a negatively. They still carried an umbrella each as a part of their trekking kit, including a torch, some eatables, and a few spare water bottles. It was also pre-decided to be in comfortable clothes and shoes as this trek was going to be a moderate one at the difficulty level.

On their right flowed the Parvati River making constant musing that filled their heart with excitement and joy. They were all lost in their respective thoughts whereas, Shivi was constantly capturing some beautiful views with her digital camera. While all others walked towards the Barshaini Dam, Shivi paused to capture a rare bird that sat on the roadside grill to her right. She looked through the camera's viewfinder, zoomed in, and was about to click when it all went dark in front of her. It looked like something obstructed her camera lens. She kept her camera a little away and tried to look at the bird with bare eyes.

“Do you need a guide?” a man who stood in front of her camera uttered. He carried an extremely outdated short spike hairstyle and wore a square-shaped spectacle that looked decades old. His thin body gave the hint that he was in his mid-twenties, but he looked too young to be a tourist guide.

Startled and annoyed, Shivi shouted “Is this the right way to offer your service? Don’t you see I was taking a photograph?”

Listening to the loud voice, all her friends came back to her. “What’s the matter, man?” Dhruv pushed the man a little away from Shivi. “Try to talk while maintaining proper distance from a girl.” He said in anger.

“Calm down Dhruv. I guess he is a local guide here.” Jo Eun Sup tried to sort things up. “Brother, we don’t need a guide. I am a localite.” Jo Eun Sup said to the man who constantly gazed at them and left the scene.

“He stared at me as if he was about to hit me,” Dhruv uttered.

“It’s okay Dhruv. Maybe, the need for money would have compelled him to react in such a way. Their business is close to nothing in the month of September. This season witnesses many landslides in this area and generally people do not come for the trek as it goes slippery due to heavy rainfall. In such cases, new travellers always need a guide.” Rudra informed.

“But you don’t really need one as I am your guide for today.” Joe Eun Sup smiled. “Common guys, let’s not spoil our mood. We should move towards the dam.” He continued directing all of them toward the dam.

"So, Miss. Shivi, would you like to enlighten us about which way we should choose from the dam?" Rudra teased Shivi thinking she might not have much information about the two routes to reach Kheerganga.

"Sure. From here the Kheerganga trek is almost 14 kilometres. We can reach the halfway of the trek by choosing any of the two ways: one, by crossing the dam on our right that would take us through the forest route via Kalga village, and two, we can opt to walk through the route to our left that passes through Nakhtan village." She smiled as she finished.

"Eun Sup, you're fired. We don't need you as our guide any more. We have already called one from Delhi." Rudra laughed looking at Jo Eun Sup.

"Well. We will choose to walk through the way to our left. It is easy and we would get to see a lot of attractions on our way." Jo Eun Sup suggested smiling.

"I believe the way through the forest is much more adventurous and is mostly preferred while going up. While coming back, we can come through the other way." Shivi countered.

"Here goes the tough competition between two newly recruited guides," Dhruv uttered.

"Shivi, I guess Jo Eun Sup is right. As the weather is constantly changing, it may even rain. I would not choose the forest way in that case, as it may be slippery and difficult for the trek. However, we can consider coming down through that way if the weather is good tomorrow." Rudra tried to convince Shivi.

"Well. I too think the same. So, let's follow what our leader says." Dhruv winked at Shivi and they all followed Jo Eun Sup.

Eleven

13:00 IST (Kheerganga Trek)

Jo Eun Sup easily tiptoed on the rocky and slippery slanting pathway at the beginning of the trek. He moved fast with such ease as if he was walking on a smooth straight surface. Dhruv too followed him with the same pace. Shivi and Rudra were left behind and they wondered if they would be able to hook up with them throughout the trek.

The mountains and apple orchids on their left and the green valley on their right were the perfect trekking scenes they cherished. Moving ahead with such beautiful attractions was not at all tiring for them. Shivi continued clicking the pictures of every beautiful thing she saw and Rudra was moving ahead with the thoughts of his last night with Disha.

The best part of this trek was, their path to the Kheerganga was well-marked. They did not have to worry about any wrong turns as there weren't any diversions to the trek. After walking continuously for about one and a half hours, they reached Nakthan village, a small and sacred Himachali village that survived on tourists and apple orchids for its living.

Jo Eun Sup sat on a bench that was kept outside a small cafe. He ordered fresh juice for all of them and said "Fill up your body with some energy. The rest of the trek would be difficult. We have easily come halfway because the weather was in our favour. If it had been hot, the soil beneath our feet would have been slippery and we might have suffered from sunstroke because of trekking under the direct sunlight for one and a half hours."

"Damn! He is so professional." Shivi joked taking a sip of the freshly squeezed orange juice.

"Indeed, he is." Rudra smiled at Shivi's comment.

"Hahaha." Jo Eun Sup laughed. "But guys on a serious note, it's already late and we must reach the hilltop before it gets dark." He suggested.

"You are hired back for the hard labour that you're doing for us." Rudra teased. "Let's resume our trekking." He said and signalled Jo Eun Sup to take the lead.

"Sure." Jo Eun Sup got up from the bench and started his march past the Kheerganga once again.

"Rudra, would you mind if I ask you something?" Shivi asked walking beside Rudra.

"Did I ever?" Rudra replied moving ahead at a slow pace.

"Why haven't you brought Seo Yoon with you? I mean we would have got to know each other better while being on this trip." She inquired.

"Uhh…" Rudra paused and quickly tailored a reply "It's just that she has been to Kheerganga many times and she doesn't feel like visiting the same place again and again."

"Ow. That means she is picky." Shivi uttered checking her cell phone. "Crap. I lost the reception." She said.

"Don't worry, I have the network. If in case we need it." Jo Eun Sup looked back and informed.

"How does he get the network? Is he carrying a satellite phone?" Shivi asked.

"Ahm. To be a professional guide, you need to carry a satellite phone." Jo Eun Sup smiled.

"Oh, I did not know that carrying a BSNL sim card means carrying a satellite phone." Rudra pulled Jo Eun Sup's leg and they all burst out of laughter.

15:15 IST (Rudranag Temple)

A long journey becomes easy and memorable when you're travelling with your friends. In no time they reached Rudranag temple, a temple that got its name from the nearby serpentine waterfall. To their dismay the temple was closed, but finding joy in little things was Shivi's nature. She went to a nearby cafe and ordered Maggie and coffee for her friends.

"You know what? Having maggie at hill stations in such cold weather refreshes your mood." She handed over a plate full of maggie to Dhruv who stood nearby the waterfall.

"Thanks, mate. Shall I tell you something, if you promise that you won't overreact?" Dhruv whispered in Shivi's ear ensuring Rudra and Jo Eun Sup didn't get to hear what he was about to say.

"Hmm. Sure." Shivi whispered back.

"Don't move your head until I am finished." Dhruv instructed and continued "Since we have started from Kasol Park, a girl is constantly following us."

"Are you sure? I mean, I have never heard of a girl following trekkers." She murmured getting surprised.

"Yes. I am. Just when you turn around towards the cafe, on the left there is a small bridge on which the girl is standing all alone." He replied.

"Okay. I will just go and check." Shivi said and was about to move.

"Don't. We need to be double-sure before we react." He instructed. "So, let's act casual and notice her for the following trek." He continued.

Shivi nodded in agreement and moved towards the bill counter.

"Shivi, here. I just paid the bill." Rudra smiled signalling Shivi to join them at the table.

She smiled back and sat with them for the coffee.

"Eun Sup, I just had a word with the cafe owner here, he said it is supposed to rain in the next few hours. So, I was thinking if we should continue our trek tomorrow morning and stay here for tonight." Rudra informed.

"Oh, common Rudra. You know these cafe guys. They must be saying this to make some money from our unplanned night stay." Jo Eun Sup said, "And as a matter of fact, we will reach our destination in just three hours, so no point staying here tonight." He continued.

"It will be dark in a few hours. If it is going to rain, we will be reaching the hilltop late." Rudra countered.

"Don't worry Rudra. We will be safe. After all, this place is our home." Jo Eun Sup replied getting up to slip his cup into the dustbin.

"Okay. Let's continue then." Rudra stood up and signalled Dhruv to join them for further trekking.

They all moved towards the small bridge on their right. Shivi looked at the bridge carefully, but there was no girl as per Dhruv's description. She asked Dhruv in sign language if he really saw the girl. Dhruv nodded, but he too wondered where did the girl go?

Twelve

15:40 IST (Kheerganga Trek)

Standing at the bridge they enjoyed the fresh breeze that carried tiny water droplets from the waterfall on their left. Those little droplets settled on their faces and gave them the cooling touch of nature. To their right flowed the river Parvati which sourced its water from the waterfall on their left. Looking at the white foamy water that flowed under the bridge, Dhruv exclaimed "Damn this place. I wish I owned a small cafe here."

"And below the cafe, you would be willing to have a gym," Shivi uttered.

"Yeah, and this man would just eat, workout, and sleep." Rudra smiled.

"Seriously bro, you two guys are lucky that you live here," Dhruv said to Jo Eun Sup and Rudra.

"See, I have been telling you guys to come here for a trip. But you took three years to reach me." Rudra said crossing the bridge and joining the trek to his left.

"Hardly matters bro. Good things are worth the wait. Finally, we are here." Dhruv smiled and followed Rudra to the trek.

"Dhruv, it is good to see you talking to us. I thought you speak less." Jo Eun Sup said.

"No way. He speaks a lot. It's just that he was lost in someone's eyes till now." Shivi said and winked at Dhruv.

"Don't tell them." Dhruv signalled.

"Whose eyes?" Jo Eun Sup asked looking here and there and finding no one around them.

"Well. Dhruv thinks a girl is following us throughout." Shivi revealed the secret that Dhruv told her.

"What? A girl?" Jo Sun Sup asked.

Rudra too listened to the conversation carefully while climbing up.

"Yes. A fair-complexioned girl with long brown hair. She carried a backpack with an umbrella in her hand." Dhruv described the looks.

"Ah. She must be a trekker like us. Don't think you are smart enough to attract a girl who would follow you." Shivi joked and eased the matter.

"She is right. You should only focus on your girl who is waiting for you in Delhi." Rudra said wondering if the looks described by Dhruv were somewhat similar to Disha. 'I might be thinking too much about Disha and why on earth will she follow us?' he thought and carried on his trek.

"By the way Dhruv, what do you do?" Jo Eun Sup asked.

"I work in an MNC and recently I have started my own digital marketing firm," Dhruv replied.

"Oh. I guess you're an engineer." Jo Eun Sup said.

"Well, yes. I am an Engineer and my higher qualification is MBA in Marketing. But how did you guess that I am an Engineer?" Dhruv asked.

"The way you keep quiet and observe things. It's a rare quality that lies with a smart mind." Jo Eun Sup smiled.

"Smart mind. Huh." Shivi taunted trying to tease Dhruv.

Dhruv looked at Shivi and was about to utter something. "Ahgh," he cried in pain as his left foot landed in a pit hole full of mud and water.

Listening to the loud shout everyone looked at Dhruv who signalled them to look at his leg. The pit hole was deep and it engulfed his entire instep. Rudra and Jo Eun Sup quickly moved towards Dhruv, made him sit on a nearby rock, and slowly took his foot out of the pit hole.

"Pour some water on it." Jo Eun Sup asked Shivi who opened the water bottle and poured water on Dhruv's foot. Slowly the mud washed away and fortunately, there were no signs of injury.

"It's alright. Just try to get up and walk carefully." Rudra asked Dhruv not to worry and continue the trek.

Dhruv got up and slowly stood on his feet.

"Are you alright?" Jo Eun Sup asked grabbing Dhruv's left arm.

"I guess so." Dhruv tried to take small steps ahead. "It's alright. I am just feeling a little pain in my left knee, but I will manage to trek." He signalled everyone to start climbing up and followed them as they moved.

"Shivi." Dhruv called her in a low voice.

"Yeah." Shivi paused and walked ahead with Dhruv at a slow pace.

"Just don't look back. Keep walking and listen to me carefully." Dhruv instructed and continued "The girl I talked about is just a few steps behind us. She is still following us."

"What?" Shivi looked into Dhruv's eyes feeling a little afraid.

"Let's do one thing. We should stop here and let her walk to us. If she walks through us, that means she is not following us, and if she stops… you know." Dhruv suggested.

They both further slowed down their pace and waited for the girl to walk to them. A few minutes passed and the girl appeared. She paused for a second as she looked at Dhruv and Shivi, but she continued trekking and walked through them.

"Look how she stared at us." Dhruv raised his right hand towards her back and was about to say something to her when Shivi dragged him back and signalled him not to react.

"Let's keep walking. We can't make a scene here just because she is trekking around us." Shivi said and asked Dhruv to move ahead on the trek.

Dhruv gulped down his words and fastened his walk towards Jo Eun Sup and Rudra. Shivi couldn't understand Dhruv's behaviour and she too followed him at a fast pace. The girl was supposed to cross her path with Jo Eun Sup and Rudra as they were much ahead on the trek. Dhruv tried to keep up the pace and made sure he doesn't lose the girl from his sight. Suddenly the girl paused, looked back, smiled at Dhruv, and disappeared.

"Holy Shiiiitt." Dhruv carried both his hands on his head and shouted aloud.

"What's wrong Dhruv?" Shivi asked from behind while Rudra and Jo Eun Sup turned their back and ran towards Dhruv anticipating that he had a fall again.

"Did you see that?" Dhruv directed his finger toward the place where the girl disappeared. "She was right there, I followed her trek, and she… she just disappeared." Dhruv looked at Shivi and uttered with his eyes wide open.

"Who disappeared?" Jo Eun Sup asked feeling a little tensed.

"Dhruv, you just relax and have some water." Shivi handed over the water bottle and went ahead on the trek to see the girl. She couldn't find her anywhere. "Rudra, Jo Eun Sup, did you guys notice a girl in a purple dress crossing your path?" she questioned while coming back.

Rudra and Jo Eun Sup both looked at each other and denied seeing any girl.

"No one is on the trek. Since we started, it's all empty. As if we are the only one's walking." Rudra said.

"But we just saw a girl who was right behind us, we paused to let her move ahead of us and she did. After that Dhruv followed her."

"And she just vanished in front of my eyes..." Dhruv interrupted when Shivi was about to complete.

"Dalgyal Gwisin." Jo Eun Sup uttered looking ahead at the trek.

"What?" Rudra asked carrying a worried look on his face.

"Nothing. She must be a passer-by. Let's continue our trek." Jo Eun Sup signalled everyone to resume their trekking and they all moved ahead with inquisitive looks.

"At least tell us what did he utter in Korean?" Dhruv asked Rudra who constantly walked on the trek following Jo Eun Sup.

"He meant you're having hallucinations. There is nothing wrong. Let's just reach the hilltop so that you can calm down and relax." Rudra assured Dhruv that everything was fine, but in reality, he knew something was wrong.

Thirteen

16:11 IST (Kheerganga Trek)

Since they had crossed the bridge, the valley was now on their left and the hills were on their right. The tiny cafes on their pathway were all closed. This was due to the off-season and fewer footfalls on the trek.

Jo Eun Sup still led their path chanting some mantras in the Korean language. He gently rubbed his right palm against his left palm in a clockwise motion while moving ahead. Rudra followed him but did not dare to interrupt. Instead of thinking much about 'Dalgyal Gwisin', Rudra tried to divert his mind to the picturesque views of the hills.

The trek was full of sharp rocks, green grass, and slippery mud, which was enough for them to make one mistake and fall into the valley. But it also had numerous tiny waterfalls, the muse of the river that flowed down the valley, and multicolour flowers that blossomed on the hills to keep them engaged with the beauty of nature.

Dhruv was lost in his thoughts. He wondered how can it be possible for a girl to vanish to nowhere in the middle of the trek. Thinking a little more, he also realized that he was the only one who saw the girl getting disappeared, while all others made him believe that she might be a normal trekker who was coincidentally crossing paths with them.

"Jo Eun Sup is right. Maybe I am hallucinating." Dhruv looked at Shivi and expected her reaction.

"I too think so, as I did not see the girl disappearing. She walked ahead too fast. Maybe she crossed Jo Eun Sup and Rudra and they did not notice her." She spoke.

"Um Hmm…" Dhruv replied.

"Don't think much about it. Just enjoy the weather." She suggested tapping on his shoulders.

Dhruv nodded and moved ahead carefully keeping his steps on the trek that was constantly narrowing.

"Are you still feeling the pain in your knee?" Shivi asked looking at his facial expressions that changed whenever he kept his left foot on the ground.

"Yes. But I will manage to trek. I have become habitual of this pain." Dhruv replied.

"Habitual?" She asked.

"Yeah. When I was in college, I was the football team captain. One day I was participating in the finals match. In the middle of the game, I fell with my knee hitting the ground and since then I am carrying a knee with severely torn ligaments." He said expecting some sympathy.

"Wow," Shivi uttered.

"What?" Dhruv questioned while Shivi quickly ran towards the huge waterfall that was just a few steps away from them.

"Oh!" Dhruv understood that 'wow' was not for his miserable accident, but was for the waterfall.

This waterfall was on their right. It fell from a great height creating the erosion of soil from the trek. The waterlogged on huge holes that appeared because of the erosion. To help the trekkers move ahead without landing their feet on the holes, the villagers connected both parts of this trek using huge tree logs. But those tree logs were kept in such a way that only one person could cross at once.

Jo Eun Sup and Rudra had already reached the other side. It was now Shivi's turn. She took out her camera and started shooting the video of her crossing the bridge keeping one step after the other.

"Be careful," Dhruv shouted from behind.

Shivi looked behind and one of her legs drifted from the tree log. She slipped and fell into the water holes on her right. It was fortunate that she did not fall into the valley onto the left, but all her clothes including her camera went wet.

"Hahaha." They all laughed at Shivi teasing her while she got up completely dripped in mud and water.

"You morons." She angrily ran towards Rudra and Jo Eun Sup showing them her muddy hands.

Rudra and Jo Eun Sup tried to cover their faces with their palms but Shivi tickled them to get their hands off their faces. She laughed aloud after cunningly rubbing her muddy hands on their cheeks. As soon as she was done, she hopped towards Dhruv who had just arrived from the other side.

"You need to take care of your camera first," Dhruv suggested handing over the camera to her.

"Oh! Yeah." She quickly snatched the camera from his hand and took out a dry cloth from her waterproof backpack. Switching off her camera, she wrapped the cloth around it and kept it inside her bag. "I hope it gets dry soon." She spoke.

"It's important for you to get dry first. Else you will catch a cold." Rudra said.

"Don't worry. I will be alright." Shivi hurriedly fetched some mud from the ground and poured it on Dhruv's arms.

"You need to increase your height to reach my face." Bending a little backward, Dhruv held her hands as she jumped to pour the mud on his face.

After trying a lot, Shivi finally gave up and moved towards the waterfall to fill up her water bottle.

"This is the last waterfall of this trek. Fill up your water bottles if you need to." Jo Eun Sup informed washing the mud from his face.

Fourteen

17:06 IST (Kheerganga Trek)

The caravan was still on the trek, moving ahead constantly towards the Kheerganga hilltop. They acted like a silent group that occasionally buzzed but mostly remained busy in taking a glimpse of every amazing view offered by the hills. Shivi regretted that her camera was still wet. She wished to capture some beautiful snaps for her Instagram account, but alas it wasn't possible.

The trek was now wide enough to let two people walk together. After walking continuously for almost an hour, Jo Eun Sup broke the silence. "The hilltop offers an amazing view of the sunset. Most of the trekkers reach the hilltop before the sunset, but they barely enjoy the beautiful view."

"Who cares about the sunset? Everyone wants to see the sunrise, a beautiful welcome to the new day." Dhruv smiled.

"I know, but sunset marks the completion of a good day. Still, it's a matter of perception." Jo Eun Sup smiled back.

"You both are right. But people like us barely get to see the sunrise or the sunset. When we work for others, we spend most of our time in their offices. So, who cares?" Shivi shrugged.

"In that case Rudra is lucky. He gets to see both as he is free to travel every day." Dhruv said.

"Yeah. I wish my father was as rich as his father. I would have owned a hotel with a couple of staff to work for me." Shivi fantasized.

"Ah. That's the perk of being a single child of a rich father." Rudra smiled with pride on his face.

"By the way, what's your job role in your company." Jo Eun Sup asked Shivi.

"I work as a human resource manager." She replied.

"Wow. So, you select the right candidates for your company." Jo Eun Sup smiled.

"Yup." Shivi took pride in her work.

"And you said your father isn't as rich as Rudra's father. But I believe you both studied in one of the most expensive management institutes in Delhi." Jo Eun Sup said.

"Her father is a branch manager in a top private bank and her mother is a marketing manager in an MNC. Smart people like her never show their richness." Rudra taunted.

"Damn! You are lucky to have rich parents. I lost my father when I was six and my mother a few minutes after that." Jo Eun Sup uttered.

"I am sorry for your loss. I wish I was really lucky." Shivi replied with a lenten face.

"I am sorry if I hurt you." Jo Eun Sup realized something was wrong with Shivi.

"It's okay. You are a strong girl." Rudra patted her shoulder.

"Hey! What's wrong? Uh... I mean I would like to know if you are comfortable sharing." Jo Eun Sup asked feeling worried after what Rudra said to her.

"I think we shouldn't let her talk about..." Rudra was about to complete it when Shivi interrupted.

"It's fine. I should face it." She said willing to share her story.

Taking a few steps ahead she gulped down some water and started narrating her story.

"My father belonged to a typical Marwari family and my mother was from a Punjabi family. Despite having differences in their caste, culture, and rituals, they fell in love with each other. Their bonding was so strong that they fought with everyone in their respective families just to marry each other. After trying a lot to stop them, their families finally gave up and agreed to get them married for their happiness.

Two years passed and my mother gave birth to her first child, me. They both were happy to have me in their life and they pampered me with everything they could. Just when I turned nine, my happiness witnessed a full stop." Shivi paused for a moment, took a deep breath, and started narrating further.

"My mother fell in love with one of her colleagues and indulged in an extramarital affair. My father noticed the change in her behaviour, but he kept ignoring. Everything remained a secret until the day when my father finally got to know the truth." A tear dropped from her left eye, but she continued, "He lashed out at her and moved to court to file for divorce. He even asked her to leave his house, but she refused to do so until the hearings were all done.

Their daily fights and the vulgar comments from society were nothing more than a mental trauma for me. Slowly, I succumbed to depression following the migraine attacks. Looking at my worsening condition, the court finally separated my parents and suggested that they take care of me one by one every six months.

I got divided between my parents, but I never liked staying with my mom. How could I see some other man cuddling my mom in front of my eyes?" The anger reflected on her face. "I hated being called her daughter, but the relationship that God created couldn't be forgotten. Days passed and I was finally an adult who had to decide her fate. I chose to live with my father, who always gave me everything that I wanted." She took another sip of water and looked at her friends, who were waiting for her to complete.

"He helped me study at one of the best institutes. I passed with good grades and got my dream job and I am here today with you all enjoying my holidays." She smiled and tried to lighten the scenario.

"How is your migraine now?" Jo Eun Sup inquired.

"Yeah. Even I forgot to ask that. I remember you once blacked out in front of me in college. I drove you home and then you were fine the next day." Rudra uttered.

"I was treated by a panel of the best doctors in India, but my migraine was at such a stage that it could not be reversed. I still face such blackouts when I am under complete stress and I am totally dependent on medications. The tiny blood vessels of my eyes are so weak that I can even lose my vision any day." A gush of tears oozed out of her eyes.

Listening to this, Rudra moved a little close to her and took her into his arms. "It's okay best friend. I am always with you. You are a girl who smiled even in the darker days of her life. You can't lose the battle to such shit illness." He tried to console her giving her hope and strength.

"Yeah. I won't. And I can never until I have idiots like Dhruv around me." She tried to crack a joke to make Dhruv smile, who silently followed them.

"If I knew that a little creature like you has such a tragic story in her life, I would have never stopped you from cracking a joke on me," Dhruv replied wondering if his statement was correct and consolable.

"Really! Hats off to you Shivi. You are a warrior." Jo Eun Sup said praising her.

"That's what you become with the passage of time." Shivi smiled and continued the trek.

Fifteen

18:40 IST (Kheerganga)

"Just fifty steps to go and to our right will be the Kheerganga." Jo Eun Sup announced noticing that everyone was tired of walking and Dhruv was almost about to sit on the trek.

"Yeah, he is right," Rudra uttered looking at Dhruv who seemed to be in disbelief.

Listening to Rudra's confirmation, Dhruv stood straight and started counting the footsteps he took ahead. "One... Two... Three..." he went on counting.

"Maybe a few steps less than what he said." Rudra looked at Dhruv whose huge legs took long leaps on the trek.

"Hahaha." Shivi smiled at the joke that Dhruv struggled to understand.

"Jo Eun Sup said fifty steps for the normal human-sized legs, not for the giraffes." Rudra further stretched his joke for Dhruv to understand and they all burst out of laughter.

"Rudra, you too?" Dhruv uttered nodding his head left to right with a deep sigh as he forgot his count while listening to Rudra's joke.

"Come on, man. I just wanted you guys to cheer up." Rudra tried to make it up for Dhruv.

"I understand bro. It's okay." Dhruv gave a tiring smile.

"And here we are." Jo Eun Sup said pointing to his right.

"Wow." Shivi and Dhruv uttered in a chorus looking at the Kheerganga meadow.

They all turned right and walked further. This place looked like a vast green field surrounded by giant hills from all sides. In the centre was the pathway that slanted up towards a temple and on both sides of the pathway were the camping sites.

"Rudra, is that the temple of Lord Shiva?" Shivi pointed at the temple that was clearly visible from far away.

"Yes. And just beside that is the Parvati Kund where we can take a hot spring bath." Rudra informed. "We need to quickly book some camps for our night stay and then we can go ahead towards the temple." He continued.

"Fine. I will book the camps. Until then you guys relax at this cafe." Jo Eun Sup said pointing at the cafe on their left.

They all settled on the low-height wooden stools kept outside the cafe and waited for Jo Eun Sup to come back.

"Rudra, what is the meaning of Dalgyal Gwisin?" Dhruv asked stretching his legs to relax the muscles.

"Uh." Rudra looked here and there and continued "It's nothing. I already told you it's about the hallucinations."

"I know it isn't. If it was so, why did he chant something continuously in his native language during the trek?" Dhruv referred to Jo Eun Sup.

"Yeah. I too noticed some weird expressions on his face when he was chanting some kind of mantra. It looked like he was worried about something. Please, Rudra, tell us." Shivi insisted.

"Okay." Rudra replied and continued "Dalgyal Gwisin or egg ghost is an evil spirit that looks like an egg. It doesn't have facial features like human beings. It lives in the mountains and haunts the trekkers."

"So according to Mr. Jo Eun Sup, we were being haunted by some egg ghost. Hahaha… Come on Rudra, give me a break. I have almost thirty eggs a day in my diet. I did not know that Korean people are so afraid of eggs that they coined the term 'egg ghost'. Dhruv laughed.

"It's not a joke Dhruv. Dalgyal Gwisin is the most fearsome and deadly ghost according to Korean folklore. It moves at the speed of a blinking eye and glares at you throughout the trek. You never get to know if something is wrong, but as soon as you are alone, the creature draws closer to you and then there is no bargaining or begging for life." Rudra looked at Dhruv whose facial expression just changed from happy to fearful.

"Does that mean the girl we met on the trek was an egg ghost?" Shivi looked curious with her eyes wide open.

"The way she followed you and swiftly crossed your path, but did not overtake us made Jo Eun Sup think about her as an egg ghost." Rudra replied "But as you said, she smiled at you. It means she has facial features and technically she is not an egg ghost. So just relax and enjoy your trip." Rudra winked at Shivi who looked afraid.

"Yeah. We did not even see her after crossing the waterfall." Dhruv added.

"Maybe she is still around us and waiting for us to split." Shivi was still stuck on the same track.

"If it is so, we have a Shaman with us. He will handle the spirit." Rudra smiled.

"A Shaman?" Shivi inquired.

"Hmm. A person who has access to the world of good and bad spirits. The one who can perform rituals like exorcism and can limit the spirits from harming a human being." Rudra replied.

"You mean Jo Eun Sup is a Shaman?" Dhruv confirmed.

"Yes, and until I am here, no ghost can dare to harm you." Jo Eun Sup spoke from behind joining the conversation.

"I have never heard of a tourist guide having powers to control the spirits. I give up my job. I think Jo Eun Sup is the most suitable tourist guide for us." Shivi laughed trying to lighten the moment.

"Kamsahamnida (Thank You)." Jo Eun Sup bowed and continued "So, the camps are booked on the left side of the pathway. You guys can freshen up and we will visit the temple fifteen minutes from now."

"Okay," Shivi uttered and they all moved towards their camps.

Sixteen

19:01 IST (Kheerganga)

The camp owners at Kheerganga had set up their camps in a group of three or more. Most of the camps were quite basic whereas a few looked a little luxurious. Jo Eun Sup had booked the three most expensive camps in a row and insisted the camp owner to organise the bonfire for them during the night. The leftmost camp was taken by Rudra and Jo Eun Sup, the middle one was captured by Shivi and the extreme right one was by default allotted to Dhruv.

As planned, they all came out of their nests after fifteen minutes. Shivi looked excited as her digital camera was now properly working and she could happily take numerous beautiful pictures for her Instagram feed.

The evening at Kheerganga was astonishingly breath-taking. The sky had started dimming and the tiny twinkling stars peaked out of the clouds that formed different shapes to play with the thoughts of tourists. Although, the Parvati Kund was not supposed to be open at this hour of the day, Jo Eun Sup had some special agreements with the management.

"We do not have many tourists at Kheerganga today. Due to this, the management has especially allowed you guys to take a hot spring bath this late. All thanks to me, your super guide." Jo Eun

Sup kept his head high in pride as he moved towards the temple through the pathway.

They all quietly followed him and noticed that the camps to their left and right were almost empty. Apart from themselves, the only people they could see were some localities who wandered with their pet animals.

After a brief walk, they could see the Parvati Kund on their right. Taking a few steps ahead and climbing some stairs, they were welcomed by the statue of Nandi that faced the temple of Lord Shiva. The temple had nothing fancy and looked historical. In the centre was the Shiv Linga which was constantly served with water through the water pot hung above it. The Shiv Linga was surrounded by the statues of Goddess Parvati, Lord Ganesha, Lord Kartikeya, and a tiny wooden board, which said 'Please do not touch the Shiv Linga'.

They all bowed their head and folded their hands to pray to the Almighty. Once done with the rituals, they moved out and looked at the outer wall of the temple that had the painting of Shiv Pariwar drawn over it. Just beside the painting was a huge wooden board hung over the wall. The board had some information about the importance of the place Kheerganga.

Shivi being more interested in clicking the pictures moved back towards the Parvati Kund, whereas, Dhruv being a disciple of Lord Shiva started reading aloud the information scribbled on the board "Kheerganga is an ancient holy place. Lord Shiva and his family have been residing here since the Satyuga. It is said that during Satyuga, Kheer used to flow from the streams nearby and that is when this place was named Kheerganga. With a motive to avoid a fight over the Kheer during Kalyuga, the Kheer that flowed from the streams was converted into the water with the help of Lord Parshurama. Even today, the cream of milk flows from the streams, and taking bath in the holy water of such a stream absolves all your sins. Just 60 meters away from this temple lies the cave of Lord Kartikeya where he performed austerity. From this cave, Lord Kartikeya used to travel to Mantalai. Now the cave has been closed, but pilgrims can still pay their visit. Important Information: Drinking this holy water will cure all your stomach-related illnesses. You can also carry this water to your home. Taking bath in this holy water will purify your soul."

"Gosh. I never knew this place would be of extreme importance to me. I find my Lord Shiva wherever I go." Dhruv uttered looking at Jo Eun Sup and Rudra.

"This proves that you are a true disciple of Lord Shiva." Jo Eun Sup smiled moving towards the stairs to get down.

"If you believe in God, you will find him everywhere," Rudra added following Jo Eun Sup.

"Wait, where are you guys going? We have to visit the cave of Lord Kartikeya." Dhruv shouted in excitement.

"Sorry, the cave is closed at this moment." Jo Eun Sup informed from down the stairs.

"Dammit!" Dhruv uttered in disappointment.

"Don't worry Dhruv. We will visit the temple and the cave once again in the early morning before we leave." Rudra informed and signalled Dhruv to move with them for the hot spring bath.

"That would be awesome bro. Thanks." Dhruv smiled joining them.

Seventeen

21:00 IST (Kheerganga)

Rudra and his friends gathered at the bonfire which was set up just outside their tents. The sky was covered by dense clouds all over and the cold breeze frequently flowed around the tents. The weather clearly indicated that their meeting wouldn't last long, but it hardly mattered. Bonfire, a few bottles of whiskey, and your dearest friends around you always make you carefree.

The concept of a bonfire is always attached to loud music and dance or a round of antakshari, but these guys had a different plan in their minds. They just wanted to enjoy the moment, chit-chat a little, and retire for the day.

Since the hour Dhruv had heard about the egg ghost, he was more curious to know about the Korean ghosts and the concept of Shamanism. He took a sip of whiskey and started the conversation.

"Jo Eun Sup, I would really like to know. In fact, I am curious about it… how do you guys actually deal with the ghosts." He asked.

"It's not so easy." Jo Eun Sup looked at Dhruv and smiled. "You have to take your lessons seriously, you need to understand the difference between the good and the bad spirits, and most importantly you should know how to take control of the situation." He continued.

"Ah. I get it. So, you guys help the good ones and screw the bad ones. Like you screwed the egg ghost on the way." Dhruv winked.

"I wish it was that easy." Jo Eun Sup replied.

"Has it been difficult? Like they show in Hollywood movies. The spirit takes control of the priest and then the priest dies." Dhruv smirked.

"Yes. I lost my father like that." Jo Eun Sup gulped the whiskey in his glass down his throat in one go.

"Uh… I am sorry. I never meant to…" Dhruv apologized feeling embarrassed for unknowingly hurting Jo Eun Sup.

"Gwaenchanayo (It's Okay!)" Jo Eun Sup replied. "I must tell you the story of my family and then you will get to know how dangerous an evil spirit can be."

"Eun Sup…" Rudra uttered keeping his hand on Jo Eun Sup's left shoulder.

"I can handle this, Rudra." Jo Eun Sup stood up and started walking around the chairs that circled the bonfire.

"I was just six years old when my mother conceived her second child. My father was happy and he took extra care of my mother since he got to know the good news. Being a Shaman, he didn't have much to do the whole day and that was the perk for me and my mother. We got ample time with each other as a family, until one day…" Jo Eun Sup paused.

Sipping another peg of wine, he raised his hand towards the sky and continued "The clouds that evening were similar to the clouds that are gazing at us now. It was about to rain that day. I was sitting on the terrace where my father was giving me lessons about how to confront ghosts. My mother was still in the kitchen when someone appeared at the door of our house. He shouted my father's name aloud and asked for some urgent help.

My father went downstairs and opened the door for him. He whispered something into my father's ear and my father hurriedly gathered all his holy belongings to go with him. While leaving the house he looked at me and said, 'Son, take care of your mom. She shouldn't come searching for me.' Hearing this I understood the gravity of the matter and requested him to come back soon. He nodded in a yes and left." Jo Eun Sup looked at the face of Shivi which reflected ample questions.

"I had that exact curiosity in my eyes when my father went with that man. Soon it started drizzling. I and mom waited for him for around three hours, but he did not return. She asked me to wait for her at home and wanted to go alone to find him, but I was reluctant to let her do so because of what my father had said to me. She looked worried and I couldn't stop her from going out. The best that I could do was to accompany her." Eun Sup paused to take note of the time.

"Did you find him?" Dhruv couldn't stop himself from asking the obvious question.

Jo Eun Sup looked at him and raised his wine glass. "Would you please fill it up for me?" he asked Dhruv.

"Sure," Dhruv replied and started filling the glass.

"We went to almost every house in the village, but none claimed to have seen him. Finally, an old man suggested us to check the last house in the village. They called it the last house because it was located on the outskirts and was not connected to the village at all. We went near the last house and noticed the lights of the house were on. Heading closer to one of the windows of a room, I saw my father performing an exorcism. It was being performed on a little boy. He was flying high in the air and was uttering something devilish in a masculine voice. 'Father' I shouted. He looked at me and looked back to his holy cross continuing the exorcism."

"But they say you shouldn't interrupt such things," Shivi uttered.

"Yes, that's what my mom told me at that very moment. But it was too late. The evil in the little boy looked straight into my eyes and travelled inside my body." Jo Eun Sup saw Shivi taken aback.

"It was a Black Soul, the most powerful spirit in the world. My father knew he couldn't stop a Black Soul, but he still went for the exorcism because the victim was a little boy. Hardly he knew that I and my mother would go searching for him and the evil spirit will capture my body." Jo Eun Sup paused and continued "I tried hard to not let the spirit take the control of my body, but… it jumped over my fathers' shoulders, snatched the cross from his hand, and forced it deep into his heart in front of my mom." A drop of tear dripped from Jo Eun Sup's right eye while he looked at his hands that were used against his will to kill his father.

Dhruv stood up and rubbed his hand on Jo Eun Sup's shoulder.

"It's fine Dhruv. I see it every day in my dreams. It is the reality of my life that cannot be changed." Eun Sup tried to look fine wiping off his tears.

Dhruv signalled Rudra to ask Jo Eun Sup to stop drinking and narrating the story further, but Rudra wanted Jo Eun Sup to let it out all at once. Dhruv understood what Rudra wanted and he moved back to his chair.

"My mom couldn't face the situation and her heart collapsed on the spot. That bloodthirsty Black Soul took my father, mother, and my little sibling away from me in just a few minutes. It didn't stop at only that; it moved back into the body of the little boy and killed his father and the boy too." Jo Eun Sup threw the empty wine glass away.

"I was coward enough to run away and save my life from the Black Soul. Sobbing and crying aloud, I ran towards the village. Listening to my screams, the villagers took me in and sheltered me for the night. In the morning my grandpa came to take me to his place. For months to come, he trained me to become a better Shaman than my father."

"Did you take the revenge?" Jo Eun Sup was about to complete it when Shivi interrupted.

"No. I couldn't. Initially, I thought I would stay among the people to find that spirit and control it, but I never got to confront it in the next thirteen years of my life. When I turned nineteen, my grandfather left the world and I decided to leave everything behind and move to India. I am still a coward." Jo Eun Sup sat on the chair feeling completely broken.

"You are not a coward; you are still saving lives as you saved ours from the egg ghost." Dhruv tried to console him.

"Dhruv is right. And a Shaman not only saves us from evil spirits but also from evil deeds and you have always been there for me to guide me on the right path." Rudra added.

"Come on Eun Sup, you are a good guide too," Shivi said.

"If it so, I deserve another peg of wine." Jo Eun Sup looked at the bottle of wine which was kept on a side table.

"No way." All of them shouted at Jo Eun Sup in a chorus.

The thunder roared and the clouds started pouring heavily. Everyone quickly stood up from their chair and ran towards the camps. The bonfire got washed away and the bottle of wine was left alone at the side table. Jo Eun Sup tried to run back toward the bottle, but Rudra didn't let him go. Exhausted, they all went for sound sleep keeping their cosy tents zip closed from the inside.

Eighteen

25 September 2019, 01:30 KST (The Goblin's House, Seoul, South Korea)

The goblin stood in front of a huge wall that had several picture frames hung on it. All the pictures were his memories from the past thousand years. The smiling faces in those pictures were the people who served the goblin for their entire life. Humans call them servants who worked for him generations after generations, but the goblin considered them as his family members.

No doubt a goblin is regarded as a god, but he has feelings too, just like humans. Every night he stood in front of the huge wall and remembered every good soul that accompanied him for a few years of his never-ending life. Seo Yoon was also a successor of his last male helper, but instead of keeping her in Korea for his service, the goblin set her free to let her live on her own terms.

He remembered how Seo Yoon was crazy about clicking pictures when she was a kid. A few hundred of those covered a major part of the wall. The goblin had bought her a digital camera on her fifth birthday and she left that camera with the goblin while leaving for India. She smiled and said, "Samchon (Uncle), keep this camera with you as a part of my memories and if you miss me too much, come to meet me."

Neatly dressed in his pitch-black long coat, he wanted to get clicked today just to cherish his memories. On his right was a wooden almirah where the camera and a tripod were kept. With all the superpowers he possessed, he never had to move an inch to make things happen. Raising his right hand towards the almirah, he bent two of his fingers signalling the doors to open. The doors went wide open and then he moved his hand from right to his front. The tripod came out of the almirah and adjusted itself in front of the goblin. He again moved his hand to the right and commanded the camera to come out of the almirah and set up on the tripod. The camera did as he commanded.

"Heyaa! Dokkaebi. (Hey! Goblin.), quickly stop your cheap magic tricks and take me to India now." The grim reaper shouted from behind entering the goblin's house without any formal permission.

"Haisshhh… Jeosung Saja (Grim Reaper), do you have manners or not?" The goblin frowned.

"We don't need manners, to tell the truth. Your magic was really very cheap." The grim reaper said looking into the goblin's eyes.

The angry and frustrated goblin shined in a blue flame and a sharp long sword appeared in his right hand. Looking at his sword, the grim reaper took a back and said "I Uh… I was kidding. I needed urgent help so I entered your house without ringing the bell".

The goblin stood still and kept looking at the grim reaper. While the grim reaper felt embarrassed, the goblin smiled and the sword disappeared. "Even I was playing a prank on you." He said keeping his hand on the grim reaper's shoulder. "Come on, let's take a picture together." He continued.

"Ah! Ne. (Yeah! Sure.)" The grim reaper bowed a little and turned towards the camera.

Smiling, they both stood in front of the camera and the goblin uttered "Hana dul set, click (One, two, three, click)", but the camera shutter did not make any sound. The goblin looked at the grim reaper and said "Smile wider, the camera doesn't want to click an embarrassed face".

The grim reaper shook his head upside down and showed his teeth.

"Let's try now." The goblin again looked at the camera and counted "Hana dul set, click (One, two, three, click)", but the camera shutter again did not act as per his command.

"I believe you need to remove the lens cap first." The grim reaper signalled goblin to take a look at the camera.

"Mwo? (What?)" The goblin looked at the camera and realised that he forgot to remove the camera lens cap before trying to click the pictures. "Heyaa! I knew the lens cap was on. I was just checking if a grim reaper knows how to use a camera." The goblin tried to cover up his embarrassment.

"Um. Hmm." The grim reaper taunted.

"You tell me, why do you need my help to go to India? You could have gone by airplane." The goblin changed the topic.

"Well. I have got some urgent assignment of collecting some souls from India and I have to reach there before they run out wandering." The grim reaper replied.

"Wait! You have got the death cards? Is it?" The goblin asked if the death cards had the name of Rudra.

"Aniyo. (No)." The grim reaper replied.

"Then his friends?" The goblin's eyes went wide open with concern.

"You know I cannot reveal the names to anyone. This is the rule." The grim reaper said.

"Show me the death cards." The goblin snatched the death cards from the grim reaper's hand and tried to look at the names, but they were all blank.

"No one except a grim reaper can see the names on the death cards. Will you take me to India now?" The grim reaper pointed his index finger toward a painting on his left.

"Ne. (Yes)." The goblin replied moving towards the painting.

24 September 2019, 22:30 IST (The Yoon's Café, Kasol)

The goblin and the grim reaper entered a room at the Yoon's Cafe.

"You should at least tell me before you get inside the painting. I always have to run behind you at the last moment." The grim reaper said taking deep breaths.

"Huh. What's new in this? You always run behind people at their last moments." The goblin said being seated on a huge white sofa that was kept inside the room.

"Maybe, I will witness your final moments too." The grim reaper murmured moving towards the bed.

"You haven't come to India to sleep. Ga Ja (Let's go), we need to collect the souls and get back to Korea as soon as possible." The goblin said worrying about the names in the death cards. He wondered if the death cards had the names of Rudra's friends. If it was so, he would have a tough time facing Seo Yoon for not telling her the truth.

"It's not the time yet. I hope you have paid the rent for this room." The grim reaper said lying on the bed yawning.

"Heyaa! Jeosung Saja (Hey! Grim Reaper), I own this hotel, okay. It's just that I have given it to Seo Yoon as a token of love." The goblin informed proudly.

"Mwo? (What?)" The grim reaper uttered.

"Eo (Yes) and the room we are sitting in is a permanently booked room for me." The goblin mentioned further.

"Huh. The perks of having an endless life." The grim reaper taunted trying to sleep.

"You also have an endless life, still you survive on the money that people leave on the graves. Haaah." The goblin taunted back.

The grim reaper did not reply and his snores started hitting the goblin's eardrums. Feeling irritated by the loud snores, the goblin took out some cotton buds from the drawer of the centre table kept in front of the sofa and plugged them in his ears. Lying down on the sofa, the goblin wondered about the names in the death cards and tried to go to sleep in order to curb his worries.

Nineteen

24 September 2019, 11:00 IST (Kheerganga)

The loud roar of the sky had stopped after thoroughly washing everything in the meadow. All the tents were zip closed from the inside and at their entrances slept the pet dogs and puppies of the tent owners to safeguard the visitors and the tents from suspicious things. Rudra, Jo Eun Sup, and Dhruv had slept as soon as they went inside their tents, but Shivi choose to sleep a little later as she wanted to check the photographs she had clicked from her digital camera.

She sneaked behind two blankets to set aside the freezing cold, but her face still peaked out of the blankets and her left hand held the camera loosely. For the first few minutes she tried not to sleep without giving a glance at all the photographs, but finally, she decided to give up. Half asleep she looked at the zip of the tent to ensure it was properly closed. After that, she looked at all the sides of the tent to check for open gaps. She smiled when she made sure that the tent was properly packed from all sides and the cold air couldn't enter inside.

She laid down on the mattress and was about to hide behind the blankets again when she noticed a shadow that appeared from behind the zip-closed tent flap. It looked like a dog. She sensed that the dog must be sleeping just outside the tent to get the warmth of the human sleeping inside. She smiled again and hid behind the blankets to catch her sleep.

11:45 IST

Shivi slept comfortably inside the tent. The camera that she held in her left hand was now a little away from her reach. The cornea of her eyes moved inside her eyelids from right to left and left to right. It seemed as if she was witnessing a dream. Suddenly she heard the sound of a camera flash. She wanted to open her eyes, but she thought her finger might had touched the flash button accidentally and she decided not to disturb her sleep.

A few minutes passed and the camera started flashing frequently. The noise and light of frequent flashes drew away Shivi's sleep. She woke up and looked at her left hand, but to her surprise, the camera was lying a few inches away from it. Picking up the camera, she wondered how it could be possible for a camera to open the shutter and click images on its own.

She started scrolling the images that were clicked during her sleep and found all the images were blank. Considering this as a technical fault, she kept the camera aside and tried to go back to sleep. While lying down she was processing the pictures in the back of her mind and realised that one of the images had a shadow-like figure in it. Quickly getting up, she looked at all the images once again and found the suspicious one.

This image vaguely showed a thin shadow belonging to a human being, possibly a girl with long untied hair. Shivi wanted to inspect the camera now. She opened the camera shutter and faced it toward the zip flap of the tent. Looking into the viewfinder, she clicked the flash button again and her heartbeats went up when the shadow appeared much clearer this time.

Hurriedly keeping the camera away, she looked at the zip flap with naked eyes. Someone was there and it stood right in front of the tent. The goosebumps on Shivi's hands rose up. She wanted to shout, but chose to keep quiet thinking the girl at the door might be sleepwalking. Shivi kept quiet and waited for her to go away.

As expected, the shadow about turned in a few minutes and started disappearing. The curiosity went at its peak in Shivi's mind. She quickly took out the torch from her backpack and kept her mobile phone in her trousers' pocket. Unzipping the tent flap, she quietly moved out and looked at the tents nearby. It was complete silence all around with no human activity seen or heard.

The dense clouds in the sky played hide and seek with the moonlight. The fog covered the grassland and visibility levels went down with the dropping temperature. Shivi tried to look as far as possible to locate the girl and she was able to grab the slightest glimpse of her walking toward the trek. "Stop" Shivi wanted to shout but gulped down her words thinking she might not be audible from such a distance.

Carefully taking her steps ahead and then moving towards the right, she walked for a few meters and reached the trek. On her right was the last camp of Kheerganga and on her left was the trek where the girl just went down.

Taking a deep breath, Shivi turned left and started trekking down. After a few minutes of the walk, she finally saw the girl constantly trekking ahead toward the dense forest. "Hey!! Stop." Shivi shouted but the girl seemed undistracted. "I said stop. This is not the right time to trek down." Shivi shouted again speeding up her walk.

"Shit!!!" Shivi uttered when the moon hid behind the clouds and the trek went pitch dark. Switching on her torch, she continued the walk and kept her eyes on the girl. "I think you should stop right now," Shivi shouted again with the highest pitch of her voice but received no reaction from the girl.

"She looks insane," Shivi muttered and kept walking on the trek. A few minutes passed and the moon shined bright in the sky making everything on the trek clearly visible. "What the f*uck?" Shivi uttered when she clearly saw the girl's face under the moonlight. It was the same girl who constantly followed her while she was trekking up with her friends.

Shivi paused for a moment and realised that she was driven into danger. Without taking a further glance at that girl, she quickly about turned and started trekking up as fast as she could. 'Make a runn... if you caannn.' she heard a creepy masculine voice from behind.

"Holyy Shitt!" She shouted and started running. "Thaakkkk..." a hammer-like heavy wooden log banged her head from behind and she fell unconscious on the ground.

Twenty

25 September 2019, 00:45 IST

The frequent lightning in the sky with loud crashing noise drove out Rudra of his deep sleep. With a heavy head and dizzy eyes, he looked at Jo Eun Sup who slept carefree, hugging a pillow. Feeling the urge to have some water, Rudra slipped his hand toward the water bottle on his left. Getting hold of the bottle, he got up and started sipping. 'Damn! I am sweating too much.' he murmured when he realised that his inner vest was wet.

Quietly keeping the bottle back and unzipping the tent flap, Rudra walked out to catch some fresh air. The fog was so dense that he couldn't see the dog sleeping just outside his tent and his right foot hit the poor animal. Growling in a low tone, the dog ran away and Rudra went alert before putting his steps further.

'I should stay inside the tent. It could be dangerous staying outside in such dense fog.' Rudra thought and about turned to get inside. Suddenly he heard the sound of Shivi's tent flap hitting the sides of his tent with the flow of gushing air. 'What the hell is this girl doing keeping her tent open at this late hour?' he questioned himself and moved towards Shivi's tent.

'God, she isn't here.' He whispered and went ahead to check Dhruv's tent which was sealed from the inside. "Dhruv! Dhruv!

Open the flap. Dhruv!!! Dhruv!!!" he shouted standing outside Dhruv's tent.

"What happened Rudra?" Dhruv got up and came out.

"Shivi is not in her tent," Rudra informed.

"What?" Dhruv inquired and quickly moved to Shivi's tent. "Where is Jo Eun Sup?" he asked Rudra to confirm if Shivi and Jo Eun Sup were together.

"He is sleeping," Rudra replied.

"Gosh! Then where has she gone?" Dhruv wondered.

"I don't know, but the fog is dense and it's dangerous outside with wild animals around," Rudra said moving towards his tent to wake up Jo Eun Sup. "Eun Sup, Eun Sup, wake up." he patted Jo Sun Sup's cheeks.

"Is it morning already? Let me sleep for a few more minutes." Jo Eun Sup said without opening his eyes.

"Eun Sup, it's late night and Shivi is missing from her tent," Rudra said in a loud tone.

"Muhyo (What?)" Jo Eun Sup opened his eyes and took a pause before he smiled and said "Michin Gae (Crazy Dog), she must have gone to the restroom. Now let me sleep." He closed his eyes and tried to get back his sleep.

"Guys! Look at this picture." Dhruv entered the tent with Shivi's camera in his hand.

"What picture?" Jo Eun Sup asked getting up.

"The picture that she clicked an hour ago," Dhruv replied handing over the camera to Jo Eun Sup.

"Damn! Shivi is in danger." Jo Eun Sup uttered. "And, if we don't find her. She will never come back." He said looking at all the pictures that were captured in the last hour.

"What do you mean by that?" Rudra questioned getting worried.

"The shadow in these pictures. It is a Black Soul." Jo Eun Sup said getting up on his feet and gathering everything he could to face the Black Soul.

While Rudra and Dhruv froze for a moment to digest what they heard. Eun Sup quickly gathered their Jackets and torches. "Come on! It's not the time to think." He said looking into their eyes and signalling them to follow him.

"How do we find her?" Rudra asked Eun Sup in a low tone.

"Randomly." Jo Eun Sup replied moving towards the trek.

"Wait. Randomly? We..." Dhruv looked at Eun Sup and paused without completing his question.

"We are going the right way. She did not wait for us outside the tents. And she would never go up towards the temple. So, she must be in the woods." Jo Eun Sup said reaching the last camp. "This time it's either you or me." He murmured and started trekking down.

Twenty One

01:00 IST (The Yoon's Café, Kasol)

A mobile phone kept on the side table of Seo Yoon's bed vibrated. She had a very fragile sleep. Quickly reacting to the vibration, she got up and looked at the mobile screen that displayed 'Jo Eun Sup calling…'

"Yeoboseyo! (Hello!)" She spoke taking the call.

"Seo Yoonaa, I am not getting a proper signal here. Before the network is lost, just listen to me carefully and act wisely." Jo Eun Sup uttered in one go.

"Mu-seun-il-i-seeo-yo? Gwaenchanayo? (What's the matter? Are you alright?" Seo Yoon asked getting worried.

"Anniyo (No). Shivi is missing and we are trekking down to find her. A Black Soul… (voice breaks). Just bring help…" Jo Eun Sup tried to complete it, but he lost the signal and the call got disconnected.

As soon as the call got disconnected, Seo Yoon rushed towards her almirah and took out the special perfume. Pouring the perfume drop after drop on the painting and keeping her eyes closed, she whispered the goblin's name. Unlike the last time, the goblin appeared in front of her, but without the blue flame.

"Seo Yoonaa!" The goblin called Seo Yoon's name.

"Sumchon (Uncle)." Seo Yoon opened her eyes and continued "Sumchon (Uncle), they are in danger and they need our help. Let's quickly go there." She grabbed the goblin's left arm and started walking towards the door of her room.

"Wait." The goblin did not move an inch stopping Seo Yoon from moving ahead. "Who is in danger and where do we need to go?" he asked.

"Rudra and his friends." Seo Yoon said trying to drag the goblin towards the door.

"Okay. Okay. We will go there, but not alone. There is someone who needs to go with us." The goblin looked into Seo Yoon's eyes and signalled her to calm down.

Before Seo Yoon could react any further, the goblin vanished into the painting and came back with the grim reaper.

"Aigo! Jeosung Saja (Oh! My God, the Grim Reaper)." Seo Yoon shouted while her face turned pale. "Is any of them already dead?" She asked, but the grim reaper just looked at her not uttering a single word. "Sumchon! (Uncle!), if anything happens to Rudra, this grim reaper will have to take me as well." She looked at the goblin shedding tears of fear and worry.

"Anniya (No). There is nothing like that." The goblin replied. "He is just with us to take the Bulack Soule to Korea." He lied looking at the grim reaper and signalling him not to reveal the truth.

"Ne (Yes.) He is right." The grim reaper said when Seo Yoon looked at him expecting him to verify the goblin's statement. "Actually, that Bulack Soule is on the list of missing souls. My higher authorities have recently assigned me the task to capture this missing soul and present it in front of them." He added.

"A missing soul?" Seo Yoon expected him to elaborate.

"Do we have time to talk about it?" The grim reaper asked raising his eyebrows.

"I think we should reach the trek first." The goblin said. "Let me find a painting on the trek." He patted Seo Yoon's shoulder and moved inside the painting.

"Wait." Seo Yoon shouted when the goblin had already left.

"What happened?" The grim reaper asked her.

"You both can travel through paintings, but what about me? How will I reach the trek?" She asked.

"Don't worry. He can even carry a human being through the paintings." The grim reaper replied.

"Thank god." She whispered and waited for the goblin to come back.

Twenty Two

01:10 IST (Kheerganga Trek)

Jo Eun Sup speedily continued trekking down chanting some mantras in the Korean language. Carefully keeping every step ahead on the trek, he signalled Dhruv and Rudra to walk right behind him.

"Shiviii" "Shiviii" Dhruv and Rudra shouted, but all went in vain as they did not find any clue of Shivi and the Black Soul.

"Why on earth is this Black Soul behind us?" Dhruv asked.

"A Black Soul encounters you only when it has a purpose." Jo Eun Sup replied.

"What purpose?" Rudra asked.

"Only the Black Soul can tell this." Jo Eun Sup replied.

'Help me…' a distant voice from down the trek distracted their conversation. Jo Eun Sup snappily looked ahead on the trek and found a thick layer of black smoke approaching them.

"It's coming." Jo Eun Sup whispered and raised his voice to chant his mantras as loud as possible. "No," he yelled when Rudra quickly covered Eun Sup and Dhruv by moving ahead on the trek.

"You have to kill me first," Rudra shouted constantly moving toward the black smoke, but the smoke went thinner as Rudra moved closer to it.

"That's impossible." Jo Eun Sup uttered when he noticed that the black smoke vanished as soon as Rudra tried to touch it.

'Help me…' Before they could move or say anything else, they heard another call for help from close by.

"She is right here." Rudra ran down the trek towards a torchlight that blinked from just a few steps ahead. Dhruv and Jo Eun Sup quickly followed him and found Shivi lying beside a huge tree.

"Shivi. Wake up Shivi." Rudra patted Shivi's cheeks.

Shivi opened her eyes and her whitish pupils went red with a blink. She cried "Rudra, please take me back home. I don't want to die." and her eyes shed blood instead of tears. Rudra took aback looking at the blood on her cheeks that fell on his hands. Before he could react, Shivi laughed and jumped on the tree.

Hanging upside down on the tree on one leg, in a blended voice of a male and a female she uttered "CATCH!" and jumped on her head hitting the ground.

Everybody's feet froze. This happened so real quick, that their brains couldn't process whatever they just witnessed. Shivi was no more among them. She was brutally killed by the Black Soul, the evil that has been chasing them since they started their journey to the Kheerganga. And the worst part was, they did not know why?

A weird silence surrounded the atmosphere. The clouds gathered and tried their best to wash away the tears of those three friends of Shivi who couldn't protect her.

Dhruv gathered some strength to move towards Shivi's body and cover her head with a handkerchief. Rudra sobbed hard but there was nothing he could do to bring her back. Bending on his knees, Jo Eun Sup paid his respect to the departing soul of Shivi.

"Can you see her?" Rudra murmured.

Jo Eun Sup nodded his head upside down looking at Shivi's holy soul that stood right in front of him with tears in its eyes.

Rudra wanted to say something, but he gulped his words down his throat.

"Let's move from here." Jo Eun Sup signalled Rudra and Dhruv to keep trekking down.

"Can't go without her." Dhruv cried.

"She wants us to leave from here right now." Jo Eun Sup uttered looking at Shivi's soul.

"Why?" Dhruv shouted at Jo Eun Sup.

"Because it is now coming for us." Jo Eun Sup replied.

"Let it come. If this is how we are supposed to die, then let's die." Dhruv uttered.

"And never try to know the reason why it killed Shivi?" Jo Eun Sup asked and started trekking down.

"I will come back for you my friend," Dhruv whispered looking at Shivi's body when Rudra grabbed his hand to follow Jo Eun Sup.

Twenty Three

01:40 IST

The rain, darkness, and memories of Shivi made it difficult for them to move ahead on the trek. None of them could believe that their only excursion together would turn into a sorrowful memory for the rest of their life.

Jo Eun Sup had no energy left to chant his mantras anymore. It looked like the Shaman had surrendered to evil. He was being followed by Rudra who constantly cursed himself for inviting his friend on this trip. It was the time when he genuinely realised how he screwed his true relationship with Seo Yoon for a stranger like Disha. He wondered if he would be alive to meet Seo Yoon ever again.

"Dhruv?" Rudra looked back and noticed that Dhruv was not moving. Dragging his hand with full force, Rudra tried to take him ahead but Dhruv did not move an inch. "What's wrong with you?" Rudra asked leaving his hand.

"Let's play a game," Dhruv uttered in a demonic voice. "If you find me, I will leave Dhruv's body." He continued and started running down the trek.

"Dhruv… Dhruv… Just don't let the Black Soul control you. You have to fight with it." Jo Eun Sup shouted from behind.

"Hahaha… He should fight? Just like you fought when you were a kid?" The Black Soul chuckled. "And I still managed to kill your entire family." It shouted from ahead using Dhruv's vocal cords and keeping the run on.

Jo Eun Sup's eyes went damp listening to what the Black Soul just said. His legs shivered and he fell to the ground.

"Eun Sup. You don't have to be weak again. Not now buddy. It's time to fight. We have to save Dhruv and take this bloody Black Soul into control." Rudra said patting the cheeks of Jo Eun Sup, who almost went unconscious.

Nodding in a yes, Jo Sun Eup took Rudra's support to get back on his feet. Taking the holy cross in his right hand and a bottle of holy water in his left hand, Jo Eun Sup ran behind Dhruv chanting his mantras loud and clear.

01:55 IST

The chase went on for a brief period of time. The man of God was behind the evil. After running for a while, Jo Eun Sup and Rudra found Dhruv standing still just a few meters away from them. They slowly moved ahead toward him.

Keeping the holy cross in front, Jo Eun Sup commanded the Black Soul to leave Dhruv's body, but with every mantra he chanted, the Black Soul went more aggressive and furious. Making a turn towards Joe Eun Sup, the Black Soul looked into his eyes and laughed.

"I won't leave his body. We are about to jump." The Black Soul signalled at the four feet jump that was required to continue the further trek.

"Nooo." Rudra and Jo Eun Sup shouted in a chorus, but all they could hear back was the sound of Dhruv's cracking knees.

For a moment, Dhruv couldn't balance his feet and lay down on his back. Wailing and thumping his hands on the ground, he tried his best to get rid of the Black Soul. Jo Eun Sup quickly jumped nearby and poured the holy water into his mouth.

"Aaaghhh… It's burning. It's burning." The Black Soul cried and rushed out of Dhruv's body.

"Rudra. Here. Before the Black Soul arrives again, let's quickly get him on his feet and try to trek down as much as possible." Jo Eun Sup whispered.

"It's not possible to trek down with broken knees," Dhruv said when Rudra and Jo Eun Sup tried to get him back on his feet.

"You have to try," Rudra uttered.

"I can't even stand. Forget about walking. You both just go and save your lives." Dhruv patted on Rudra's shoulder.

"I have asked Seo Yoon to bring help. She would be here anytime. At least try." Jo Eun Sup said to Dhruv.

"Do you really think so? The constant rain and slippery mud on the trek will never let Seo Yoon reach us before morning. Just go and leave me alone. I promise I will stay alive for you to come back and take me home in the daylight." Dhruv replied settling down and taking support of a huge rock nearby.

"I am not leaving." Rudra said. "Not without you." He continued.

"Okay. Let's wait here till the morning." Jo Eun Sup added and they both sat beside Dhruv.

Twenty Four

02:25 IST

It was a pin-drop silence all around. The rain had stopped and the fog vanished making everything clearly visible. Rudra opened his eyes and realized that he went fast asleep on the trek. Jo Eun Sup was lying beside him but Dhruv was missing. Collecting the flashback of the night, Rudra quickly assembled himself and stood up looking here and there to find Dhruv.

"Eun Sup... Eun Sup... wake up. Dhruv isn't here." He whisperingly asked Jo Eun Sup to wake up.

Jo Eun Sup stood up and carefully observed the muddy trek. Some freshly developed footprints on the trek ensured him that Dhruv was trekking down. Keeping quiet, Jo Eun Sup signalled Rudra to start following the footprints. They both kept going until a point where the further trek was connected through a bridge that was made up of three giant tree logs.

The tree logs were wet and slippery and there was nothing to grab and hold on to while crossing the bridge. Rudra and Jo Eun Sup looked at the trenches at both ends of the bridge, they were pitch dark and looked like an endless black hole.

"No wonder how people often vanish from the Kheerganga trek. If you fall into one such trench, no one will ever get the clue of your body." Rudra said.

"But we have to cross this bridge at any cost." Jo Eun Sup replied moving ahead.

"Wait." Rudra uttered holding on Jo Eun Sup's hand "Do you think Dhruv just crossed this bridge with his broken knees?"

"He didn't. The Black Soul did." Jo Eun Sup answered.

"I thought a ghost can't walk with a human body with broken joints," Rudra uttered.

"You are wrong. A ghost rather drags your body in whatever condition it is. The only aim of an evil spirit is to give you pain. Dhruv is being forced to walk ahead. His body and soul are in immense pain." Jo Eun Sup started keeping his steps ahead on the middlemost tree log of the bridge and Rudra followed him.

Carefully crossing the bridge, Jo Eun Sup further looked down at the trek to find the footprints to follow, but to his dismay, there weren't any. He wondered if Dhruv stayed behind the bridge.

"Did he?" Rudra looked at the trek and uttered. He wanted to ask if Dhruv had fallen into the trenches while crossing the bridge.

They both cautiously looked back at the bridge and wondered if Dhruv had really fallen. Giving a quick glance at the bridge, they looked ahead at the trek again.

"Are you looking for me?" Dhruv suddenly appeared in front of Jo Eun Sup and Rudra.

"Holy shit." Jo Eun Sup shouted trembling out of fear.

"Fear in the eyes of a God-man? This is the only thing that I enjoy the most." Dhruv uttered catching Jo Eun Sup's neck and picking him up to throw him into the trenches.

"Rudra, take out your locket now or I will kill him." Dhruv looked at Rudra and ordered him to do away with the locket that he wore around his neck.

Lowering his eyes towards the locket, Rudra wondered if it had something extraordinary in it. He slowly took it out and kept it in his right hand.

"Throw it into the valley, now," Dhruv shouted signalling that any delay would be life-threatening for Jo Eun Sup.

"Rudra, don't…" Jo Eun Sup murmured.

"Why?" Rudra looked at Jo Eun Sup with confusion.

"He has to. If he wants to save your pathetic life." Dhruv uttered getting Jo Eun Sup closer to the trenches.

"He doesn't…" Jo Eun Sup kicked Dhruv's chest to lose his grip and jumps away towards the trek.

Due to his broken knees, Dhruv lost his balance and fell down on the trek, but the Black Soul controlling him went more frustrated and angrier. Making several tries, the Black Soul finally got him up and made his move toward Jo Eun Sup.

"Missing Soul. Respond to my call now." The grim reaper appeared out of nowhere and commended the Black Soul to respond.

The Black Soul did pause for a second but continued towards Jo Eun Sup. Opening his mouth wide, Dhruv blurted out thick red blood on Jo Eun Sup's chest and grabbed his neck again. Before he could harm Jo Eun Sup, a blue flame pierced Dhruv's body. It was the attack of the goblin's sword.

Forced to leave Dhruv's body, the Black Soul stood right in front of the goblin. With untidy curly hair and chalk white face of a woman carrying pitch black lips with a charcoal-coloured outfit, it starred into the eyes of the goblin and asked "Who on earth are you to stop a Black Soul?"

"I am the fire, water, wind, light, and dark. I am your end." The goblin replied.

"Haah… General, is it you?… Hurhurhurhur… oh my, it looks like nothing has changed in these years. Has it?" The Black Soul looked into the goblin's eyes and wicked.

"General?" Rudra uttered.

"Let's quickly finish this chase as we did in the pasttt…" The Black Soul hurried towards Jo Eun Sup to enter his body, but before it could, the goblin's sword pierced through the Black Soul once again. Scattering into pieces, the Black Soul turned into thick black smoke and formed a circular pattern in the sky. It then moved towards Jo Eun Sup and entered his body through his nostrils.

Several attacks of the goblin's sword made the Black Soul weak. It tried its best to control Jo Eun Sup's body but it couldn't. Jo Eun Sup's soul was the purest of all. It threw the Black Soul out within seconds.

As soon as the Black Soul was out, the Grim Reaper took out his red flamed sword and signalled the goblin to attack. They both pierced the Black Soul with their respective swords and the Black Soul scattered into ashes.

A locket rolled down the trek with the ashes of the Black Soul. It was the same weird locket that Disha wore when she met Rudra for the first time in the café. Rudra bent down to pick it up. As soon as he touched the locket, he felt as if he was travelling through someone's past life. He apparently picked the locket in his hand and stood up, but his eyes could tell that he was mentally somewhere else. "Nooo…" He shouted carrying tears of regret in his eyes.

"What happened Rudra?" Seo Yoon asked getting closer to him.

Rudra bent down on his knees and cried.

"Samchon? (Uncle?)" Seo Yoon looked at the goblin carrying a question in her eyes.

The goblin slowly blinked his eyes and nodded his head upside down signalling Seo Yoon not to worry. He moved ahead and patted Rudra's shoulder "Pyeha (Your majesty) should never cry like a kid. I know what you have been through, but I promise this is the end of your sorrows" he uttered helping Rudra get back on his feet.

"Pyeha? (Your majesty?)" Seo Yoon spoke getting surprised.

"I will tell you everything but before that, let us handle the situation here." The goblin suggested.

Twenty Five

03:00 IST

Dhruv lay unconscious on the trek since the goblin's sword pierced his body. Jo Eun Sup called his name several times but he did not move an inch. "Jeosung Saja (Grim Reaper), please help him." He requested the grim reaper to do something and bring back Dhruv's consciousness.

The Grim Reaper stood beside Dhruv's body and looked at all the four death cards that he carried in his hand. Flipping the first card out of its envelope, he read "Dhruv, 26 Years Old, 'Born on September 25th, 1993.' 'Died at 02:50 IST on September 24th, 2019.' 'Cause of death, excessive bleeding due to multiple fractures.' Can you please confirm?" He raised his eyebrows and looked straight into the eyes of Dhruv's soul that stood in front of him.

Dhruv's soul nodded in a yes carrying tears in its eyes and disappeared for its journey to the next life.

The grim reaper's announcement made it difficult for Jo Eun Sup, Rudra, and Seo Yoon to hold on to their tears. They sobbed hard having their own regrets in mind. While Rudra regretted bringing Dhruv on the trip, Jo Eun Sup regretted that he couldn't save his life and Seo Yoon wondered if such a cheerful human deserved a painful death.

The grim reaper about turned and read the second card "Shivi, 27 Years Old, 'Born on April 20th, 1992.' 'Died at 01:35 IST on September 24th, 2019.' 'Cause of death, internal bleeding in the skull due to fall from a great height.' Do you confirm?"

Shivi's soul that had just arrived nodded in a yes and moved towards Jo Eun Sup who was praying for the departing souls. "Eun Sup, please tell my dad that I loved him and would want him to be my father in my next life." She uttered as she knew Jo Eun Sup could see her.

Listening to such words from Shivi shattered Jo Eun Sup from the core of his heart. He shed tears and his eyes blinked in affirmative.

"Thank you, Eun Sup." Shivi said slowly turning into a white flame that flew towards the endless sky.

The grim reaper still had two cards that were to be read. He moved towards the goblin and handed over the third card to him. Although the goblin couldn't read the name on the death card, he knew whose name was scribbled on it. Looking at Rudra and Seo Yoon, the goblin raised a blue flame on his right hand and put the card over it. Soon the card caught the fire and blew into the air forming golden ashes.

"Whose name was there on the card?" Seo Yoon asked.

"Rudra." The goblin replied.

His reply left them all terrified. Before any of them could ask why did the Black Soul chase them, the goblin chose to break the momentary silence and said, "Rudra, you were supposed to die tonight, but you're very fortunate to come across a soft-hearted deity. I just don't feel like watching any more deaths tonight."

"Joesonghabnida Samchon (I'm Sorry Uncle), I shouldn't have cheated on Seo Yoon. I regret entertaining Disha that night." Rudra bent on his knees and folded his hands in front of the goblin.

"Please get up." The goblin helped Rudra get back on his feet and continued "In your previous life, you were my King and I served you as a General. You have taken birth as a different human being but for me, life has been eternal as I never died since then. I cannot see you bent on your knees in front of me. As far as Disha is concerned, even if you had tried, you wouldn't have been able to avoid her coming to you. Because she is connected to your past life."

"Samchon (Uncle)?" Seo Yoon curiously looked at the goblin.

"Seo Yoonaa, Disha was a Black Soul that survived a thousand years hiding from the grim reaper and chasing the King. Whenever the King took a new birth, Disha killed him and hid back in the darkest corners of the earth. It was supposed to kill the King today and in his next life as well. But this had to end someday. I'm relieved, it did." The goblin answered her unasked question.

"But why? Why was the Black Soul behind the King?" Seo Yoon inquired.

Taking a deep breath, the goblin started narrating a story.

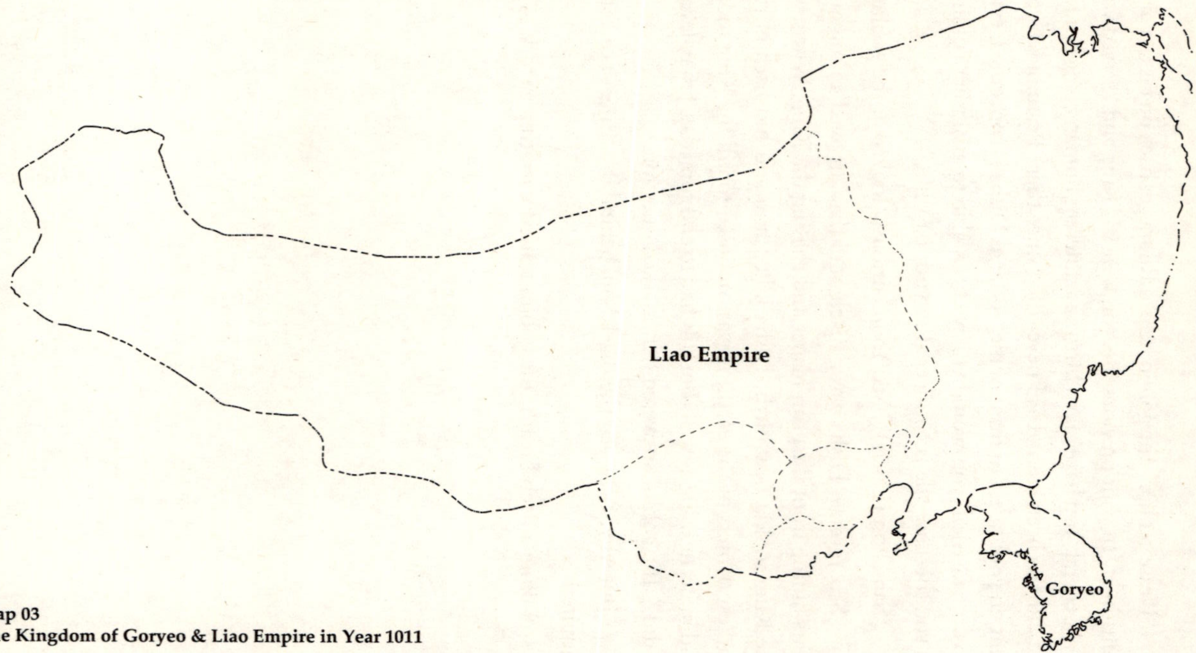

Map 03
The Kingdom of Goryeo & Liao Empire in Year 1011

Twenty Six

The Year 1011 (The Kingdom of Goryeo)

This story dates back to the Kingdom of Goryeo. Wang Yi was crowned as the king because he inculcated the traits of a king in the early stages of his life. He was a generous emperor. Be it a common man walking on the street or a courtier working closely with him, everyone praised his style of ruling the country. This was all possible because he treated his people like his own family. Securing the country from outside attacks and providing the necessary livelihood to every individual was his priority.

Apart from being a good human by heart, he was a great warrior as well. Whenever he received a threat from a nearby kingdom, he always chose to be the first one to attack. Be it the unfavourable weather conditions or a huge army at the other end, he never got afraid of anything when he was on the war field. He always fought like a lion and came victorious with flying colours.

His weakness was his love for queen Do Yoon. He often left the courtroom early just to spend more time with her. Though the queen couldn't conceive and give birth to the heir of the kingdom, Wang Yi's love for her never faded. Despite getting several suggestions to go for a second marriage, the king considered Do Yoon as his only wife.

Time passed and the king's health suddenly started deteriorating. Several doctors from Goryeo stayed at the palace to monitor the king's health every few hours. The Kingdom of Goryeo faced a hard time. I being the General of the kingdom received orders from the king to attack any country that threatened to open war against Goryeo.

Several months passed, and I remained at war. When one war ended, the other started. I did not get a chance to see the king, but I received orders from him through the royal messenger. His health of course, did not improve, but his will to live more was commendable. Killing people became my daily routine. My hands could never get off the blood of those enemy soldiers who fought for the greed of their king.

Some of them fought bravely while some cried on their deathbed realising that they would never get to see their family ever again. I could see the pain in their eyes, but I was bound to safeguard my country in the absence of my king at war. After fighting for over a year, we finally gained victory over all the enemies of Goryeo. I went back to the kingdom with the good news. The king held me in his arms and rewarded me with a royal house to live in.

While coming out of the palace, I caught hold of a suspicious messenger on his way to the queen's room. He carried a letter along with some powder cubes that he was willing to deliver to the queen. Upon asking him several times about his identity, he told me he was a secret messenger hired by the queen. Handing over those powder cubes and the letter to me, he requested me to secretly deliver them to the queen. As soon as I moved towards the queen's room to deliver those belongings, the messenger committed suicide by gulping some poison pills.

I quickly sensed that some conspiracy was being weaved by the queen along with an outsider. I decided to not deliver the letter to the queen and asked a royal guard to hide the dead body of the messenger until further orders. Before moving to my royal house, I gave the powder cubes to a doctor and strictly instructed him to find out the composition of those cubes. Following that, I chose to read the letter. To my surprise, it had the secret of the king's illness. It read…

"My beloved Do Yoon, we will meet on the full moon day at the royal armoury. Keep offering these sweet poison cubes to the king in doses as I prescribed you in my previous letter. This poison will not kill the king, but won't let him be fit again. Soon the day will arrive when the king will be totally incapacitated to think or move. That will be the day when you will be given total control of the kingdom, and we can happily marry each other, eliminating the king from our lives forever. Yours and only yours, Hong Min."

Without wasting a second, I visited the doctor whom I had instructed to find out the composition of those powder cubes. He verified that those powder cubes were made up of sweet poison imported from our neighbouring country Liao.

Moving to the king's room, I ordered the royal guard to present the dead body of the messenger before the king. He did as I ordered.

"Please read this letter Pyeha (Your majesty). This messenger was about to deliver it to the queen." I handed over the letter to the king.

He silently read the letter and looked at the dead body of the messenger. Before he asked me anything, I called for the doctor to move inside the room and tell him about his research on powder cubes. After verifying all the facts, the king ordered me to keep this incident secret until the day of the full moon. He also asked me to deliver the poisonous cubes and the letter to the queen, telling her that a secret messenger had left those for her.

For the next few days, the king remained lost in his own chain of thoughts. Despite knowing the fact that he was being served poisonous food by the queen, he kept having it gladly. Maybe, he thought the queen still loved him and would stop poisoning him. But alas, it did not happen.

A week passed and then arrived the full moon day. As expected, in the afternoon, the queen secretly moved to the armoury. There stood a tall man who carried long moustache and a beard on his face.

"Oh, dear Hong Min, you can't even imagine how happy I am seeing you after a long time. Trust me, my love for you never faded an inch since we first met in Liao, our own country." The queen said, hugging the man.

"I know, Do Yoon. It's just a matter of few more days and then we won't have to meet secretly like this." Hong Min replied, caressing the queen's hair.

"I can't wait anymore. What if I give the entire bunch of sweet poison to the king in one go?" the queen asked.

"The doctors looking after the king's health don't know that the king is being poisoned. This is the quality of the sweet poison if given in a very limited quantity. But if you give him the entire lot of poison in one go, things may go against you." Hong Min replied.

"Hmm. Then I will go as per our previous plan. We can't let the Kingdom of Goryeo slip off our hands." The queen uttered.

"What if I tell you the kingdom will never be yours?" The king shouted, entering the armoury.

Before Hong Min could even try to move an inch, I slit his throat and added his name to the list of people killed by my sword. The queen then started begging the king to spare her life, but the king was adamant about giving her a painful but slow death. He ordered us to hang her upside down until her last breath, but none of us dared to touch the queen. Giving up on his emotions that stopped him from killing her, the king hung the queen upside down and asked us to exit the armoury. He said he would stay with the queen till her last moment, and therefore, no one was allowed to enter the armoury until he came out on his own.

Inside the armoury, the king sat on a chair kept right in front of the queen. He looked at the queen's face which turned red due to the accumulation of blood in her facial blood vessels. "If you had told me once that you needed the kingdom, I would have gladly given control of the entire Goryeo to you. But if you think that I would hand over my kingdom to a traitor like Hong Min from Liao, you're mistaken." The king said.

"Wang Yi…" the queen was about to utter something but the king interrupted "A king lives for his kingdom and dies for the people in his kingdom. My love for you was endless, but my love for the people of Goryeo is eternal."

"Give me one more chance Pyeah (Your majesty)." The queen mumbled feeling dizzy due to excessive blood flow in her brain.

"I wish I could. But I don't trust you anymore. You made me believe that true love doesn't exist." The king cried his heart out.

"You will regret killing me." The queen frowned in rage.

"I am sure, I will." The king replied and kept looking into the queen's eyes. She repeatedly gasped to breathe as her lungs stopped absorbing enough oxygen. With every passing second, her heart slowed down and pumped a lesser amount of blood.

"You won't stay alive for long. I will come back for you." The queen uttered her last few words and her heart failed.

The king came out of the armoury and straight away moved to his room. He ordered the doctors to leave the palace, stating he would like to spend some time alone. I requested him not to let the doctors go, but he said he would call them back if required. As per his orders, the queen was declared dead due to a heart attack, and the secret of her having an affair with Hong Min was not revealed to anyone in Goryeo.

In the next few days, the king almost stopped interacting with everyone in the palace. He had the timely medications, but his health did not improve at all. It looked like he was still being poisoned, but it wasn't possible as I always checked all the dishes cooked for him.

Sometimes he could be heard talking to the queen as if she was alive. He even complained that the queen wanted him dead and was poisoning his food. People living in the palace said that the king had lost his mind, still I being the General of Goryeo had to stay with him during the hard days of his life and keep the secret of his emotional instability from the ministers and general public of Goryeo. I also ordered the ministers and the courtiers not to gather in the palace, stating that the king wanted to spend some time alone.

Inconsolable, incurable and finally the incapacitated Wang Yi took his last breath on a rainy day. It looked like the entire universe cried about losing him.

Twenty Seven

25 September 2019, 03:45 IST (Kheerganga Trek)

The goblin finished narrating a tale of bravery, love, betrayal, and the painful death of king Wang Yi. Everyone on the trek had their eyes filled with tears. Rudra remembered everything he had gone through in his past life as king Wang Yi. He regretted knowing the fact that in his previous life he longed for the true love that cheated on him and in his present life, he cheated on someone who loved him truly.

"Seo Yoonaa, you wanted to know why Black Soul was behind the king?" The goblin looked at Seo Yoon and asked, "It was the queen Do Yoon behind Wang Yi" He continued.

With her feet barely showing any movement, Seo Yoon stayed numb and gazed at Rudra, who held his eyes down with guilt.

"You don't have to regret too much about meeting Disha. Nothing happened between you and her that night." The goblin kept his left hand on Rudra's right shoulder.

"What?" Rudra, Seo Yoon, and Jo Eun Sup uttered in a chorus looking straight into the goblin's eyes.

"Eo (Yes), the Black Soul visited him in the form of a human-like body. It introduced itself as Disha." The goblin replied.

"Then why didn't it kill me that night?" Rudra asked.

"Because of your locket." The grim reaper moved into the conversation.

Rudra looked at the locket he carried. He wondered how such a simple locket could save him from the deadliest evil spirit on this earth.

"But this locket…" Rudra was about to complete when the grim reaper broke in, "Do you remember the day when your mom met a car accident and was hospitalized?" he asked.

Rudra kept quiet and nodded a yes.

"The doctors tried hard to save her but they couldn't. Within a few minutes of hospitalizing, she died." The grim reaper confirmed.

"Yes," Rudra replied.

"You tried to jump out of the window from the third floor as you were too attached to your mom and you did not want to live without her." The grim reaper again confirmed.

"Yes." Tears dripped continuously from Rudra's eyes and he went to the flashback.

04 June 2005, 20:00 IST (City Hospital, New Delhi)

Rudra's world had fallen apart seeing his mom on the hospital bed. She met with a car accident an hour ago and the doctors were trying their best to save her life. Gasping hard to breathe through the oxygen mask, his mother looked at him through the glass door of the room and worried about his mental state. He was just a teenager who couldn't do much to save his mother's life. Moreover, his father wasn't around to console him. He was in a foreign land trying to catch the earliest flight to New Delhi to reach his family.

"Get the defibrillator ready, her heart has stopped pumping." The head doctor shouted. "Here. 1, 2, 3… Once again 1, 2, 3… Once more 1, 2, 3…." The doctors tried their best to bring her heart back to the rhythm but they couldn't.

'Beep…' the heart rate monitor made a constant sound with no visible graph.

"I am sorry." The head doctor walked out of the room with his team, looked at Rudra, and left the room open for him.

"Mom. Mom… Please come back." Rudra ran inside the room and cried holding her hand but his mother was no more.

Falling short of tears, Rudra decided to give up on his life too. He wasn't willing to spend his life ahead without his mom being around him. Moving towards the window pane of the ICU room, he stood at the edge of the window and was about to make a jump from the third floor.

"Stop it!" An old lady with a wrinkled face kept her hand on Rudra's shoulder and asked him to get down.

Rudra said nothing and got away from the window pane.

"It's not the right thing my child." The old lady in a complete white attire rubbed her hand on Rudra's head.

Rudra looked at his mom's body and sobbed hard.

"Do you know what will happen to your mom's soul if you die tonight?" the lady asked.

Rudra nodded in a no.

"She would not be able to leave this world happily, and her soul would wander in pain." The lady informed. "Do you want your mom to suffer because of you?" She asked.

Rudra again nodded in a no.

"From today onwards, you have to start living her dreams. Go to the places she always wanted to, eat the food she would have loved trying, and do the work she enjoyed doing the most. This is the only way to make her soul depart peacefully." The old lady looked into Rudra's eyes and blessed him with contentment. "Here." The lady handed over a locket to him and said "Keep it around your neck always. This is my blessing for you and will keep all the evils away from you."

Rudra took the locket from the lady and wore it around his neck. The old lady smiled and vanished into thin air.

25 September 2019, 04:00 IST (Kheerganga Trek)

"Every life is touched by a deity at least once. Just when you were drifting away from the world, the deity nudged you back in the right direction." The goblin uttered helping Rudra come back to the present.

"That wrinkle-faced old lady was a deity?" Rudra confirmed.

"Of course. Human beings cannot disappear as she did." The goblin replied.

"But why did the deity choose me?" Rudra inquired.

"At the moment of her death, your mother made a wish with a powerful desire. She wanted you to live happily ever after she was gone from this world. The old lady was a soft-hearted deity who granted her wish." The goblin responded.

Rudra held back his tears and realised his mom's wish was to see him happy. He tried not to cry anymore.

"Everything that happens to human beings is just a part of the bigger plan that the almighty has." The grim reaper added.

"What does that mean?" Seo Yoon asked.

"If Rudra hadn't been doing what his mom always wanted to, he wouldn't have been to Kheerganga today. His mother was a nature lover, she always wanted to own a hotel in the hills and to go on various expeditions as you guys did." The goblin replied.

"And if he hadn't been living in Kasol, he would have never met Seo Yoon." Jo Eun Sup guessed.

"Correct." The goblin looked at Jo Eun Sup and replied.

"If I wouldn't met Rudra, I wouldn't be in India." Seo Yoon added.

"And if you weren't here, we would have never come here to save you guys from the Black Soul." The grim reaper said.

"That means it was all predestined." Rudra's uttered.

"Ne (Yes)." The goblin and the grim reaper replied.

"And why you two were destined to be here?" Seo Yoon asked.

The goblin looked at the grim reaper and said "The private messenger of queen Do Yoon who swallowed the poison pills and killed himself was punished by the almighty for taking his own life."

"The person who suicides becomes the grim reaper." Jo Eun Sup uttered.

"Ne (Yes). The messenger was sent back to the earth without having any memories of his past life. He is living as a grim reaper who doesn't have a name but he needs a home to live in and food to eat. Only to value the life and identity he had once abandoned." The goblin replied.

"I regret taking my own life. I was afraid of the punishment I would have received after being caught by the General." The grim reaper took a deep breath "I have served as a grim reaper to the almighty for a thousand years now. The department of names from where I get these death cards had recently informed me that I would be discharged from my duties as soon as I collect the last few souls from the earth and the last one to collect is the queen's soul." The grim reaper said looking at the locket of the Black Soul that laid on the trek.

"Is to collect?" Rudra gazed at the locket.

The grim reaper picked the locket from the trek and raised it high towards the sky. A bolt of lightning roared behind the clouds and ran toward the locket. Hitting the locket with all its strength, the lightning crushed it into millions of dust particles that settled on the trek.

"And here I finish my last duty as a grim reaper." The grim reaper smiled carrying tears in his eyes. "I lived as a grim reaper to know the value of my life. I travelled all the way to India to collect the Black Soul that kept hiding for over a thousand years. Maybe, I was destined to serve the queen for one last time by sending her to the almighty. And thanks to the goblin for narrating the story of Wang Yi. Before leaving this world forever, at least I got to know who I was and why did I abandon my life." The grim reaper said looking at the goblin.

"Ya Jeosung Saja (Heya! Grim Reaper), you lived well in this life as a grim reaper." The goblin patted the shoulder of the grim reaper.

"Samchon (Uncle)." Seo Yoon wanted to ask something but stopped.

"I know what you want to know Seo Yoona." The goblin smiled and took them all to the flashback.

Twenty Eight

The Year 1011 (The Kingdom of Goryeo)

King Wang Yi's dead body was laid in the palace courtyard. It was the day of national mourning. Every individual in Goryeo had tears in their eyes. Wang Yi was like a family member to each household and therefore, everyone wanted to see the king for one last time. A huge gathering stood outside the palace, but the ministers and courtiers stood right beside the king's body and strictly ordered the royal guards not to let anyone enter the palace.

"General, the royal doctor told us about the king's emotional disbalance in his last few days. We have also got to know that you kept his severe illness a secret from us as well as the public. You did not let us keep the court hearings stating that the king wanted to spend some time alone. Why did you do that?" One of the ministers asked.

I stood right in front of the ministers and courtiers. Thinking about all the possible reactions that I could receive from their end, I answered "If I would have let anyone in the Goryeo know about our king's severe illness, no doubt the word would have spread faster than the fire in the woods. In no time, our enemies would have formed a cartel and attacked us. Would you ever let your kingdom be in danger just because your king required more time to recover from his sadness?"

"Huh. Now you name it sadness." The other minister taunted.

"Pyeha (Your majesty) was extremely sad since he lost the queen. He was emotionally broken, so he was not recovering well." I tried to clarify.

"The queen that poisoned the king for months to snatch the kingdom and hand it over to a traitor like Hong Min. What kind of king would be sad losing such a queen?" The minister asked.

I looked at the team of doctors and royal guard whom I had asked to keep Hong Min's assassination and the queen's disloyalty a secret. They kept their heads down in front of me, feeling guilty for not being able to keep the secret.

"You guys couldn't keep the integrity for your king? What kind of royal doctors and guards are you?" I shouted at them with anger and concern.

"Shouting at the doctors and guards won't hide your mistakes General." The other minister raised his voice.

"Ya! Minister. Do you know whom are you questioning? I did my best to keep the kingdom safe." I spoke.

"Or maybe you wanted the king to die. So that you could get control of the kingdom." The minister doubted my loyalty.

"Is this what you think of me after I fought endless battles for Goryeo? I killed thousands of enemy soldiers to protect the country even when Pyeha (Your majesty) wasn't well." I asked.

"That is what concerns us more. After every battle you won, the people of Goryeo worshipped you as if you were the king. That's what made you greedy and you eliminated the king by not letting us know about his severe illness." The other minister uttered. "If you had told us about his severe illness, we would have called for specialist doctors from ally countries." The minister added.

"Doctors from ally countries? Name a country that has a team of doctors better than ours. If the doctors from Goryeo couldn't cure the king, I bet no one on earth would have. Pyeha (Your majesty) wanted to be alone. He needed emotional support and I was there for him every second of his hard time." I shouted.

"You remained with him to make his health more miserable. The truth is, you killed the king. We want you executed." The minister shouted back.

As soon as the minister said this, the entire army of Goryeo stood around me and aimed their weapons against me. I kept quiet and wondered if these were the people for whom I fought endless wars on the battlefield. The minister moved ahead and drew my sword out from the sheath that I carried around my waist. Holding it high before my eyes, he moved and ran it sharply behind my knees. I could barely stand and finally went down on my knees.

"Head down, you traitor." The minister shouted and everyone in the palace repeated after him.

I carried pride in my eyes but did not keep my head down. I was a proud and loyal General to my king and the kingdom of Goryeo. There was nothing I was ashamed of. I served my country like a warrior and I wanted to die like one. I kept my head high until the minister rammed my own sword into my chest. I lay on the floor, bleeding and crying.

The minister asked the royal guard to open the palace doors for the general public. He announced my name as a traitor of Goryeo and the murderer of king Wang Yi. The entire nation cursed me.

"No one shall retrieve the traitor's dead body. Leave it in the fields so that animals can feed on it." The minister ordered and I was thrown into the barren land of Goryeo. The sword was still in my chest, and I wailed in pain.

Twenty Nine

25 September 2019, 04:25 IST (Kheerganga Trek)

The goblin silenced for a while and felt a squeezing pain in his chest.

"Samchon, Gwenchanayo? (Uncle, are you alright?)." Seo Yoon moved toward the goblin and asked.

"Gwenchana (I am fine)." The goblin replied. "It's just that I still feel the pain of the sword in my chest when I try to remember that day." He continued.

"That day did anyone approach for your help." Jo Eun Sup asked hesitantly.

"Anniyo (No). Hours passed, and I felt thirst, hunger and pain. People of Goryeo who trusted me did gather around me but did not dare to help with anything except praying the god for my painless departure from this world." The goblin replied. "'May the soul of brave General rest in peace.' 'Dear almighty, bless the General's soul.' People shouted and cried. 'Do not pray to anyone. No one is listening.' I replied." The goblin added.

"But you said you did not die. You are living the same life." Rudra uttered.

"I did die. Just when the sun shone the brightest in the sky, I died carrying my sword into my chest." The goblin said.

"But..." Seo Yoon was about to complete when the grim reaper uttered, "When a powerful desire indwells in things touched by mortal souls, they become Goblins."

"What does that mean?" Seo Yoon asked.

"That means he returned because his sword was enchanted with a powerful desire. The desire to live." Jo Eun Sup confirmed.

"Yes. The almighty held me responsible for killing thousands of enemy soldiers whose blood was on my sword and some of them were even the descendants of deities. He sent me back to the earth, stating that I would be immortal and watch my loved ones die. I received my life back as a reward for protecting the people of Goryeo, but it is also my punishment as I couldn't forget the death of people who served me in the last thousand years." The goblin spoke.

"Did you take your revenge on the minister?" Rudra asked.

"Anniyo (No). The people of Goryeo did. I just threatened the minister that I would kill him if he didn't tell the truth to the public." The goblin replied.

"The truth?" Jo Eun Sup questioned.

"King Wang Yi did not have a child of his own. Therefore, there was no heir to the kingdom after he was dead. In such situations, the closest relative of the king who possesses leadership qualities is chosen to be crowned as the new king. Until a new king is crowned, the control of the kingdom remains with the Yangbans (Highly educated civil or military officials during the Goryeo dynasty). I being the general was at the topmost of the hierarchy, and the minister was next to me. He was greedy, and he wanted the powers in his hands. He conspired to get me killed. Blaming that I was a traitor and a threat to the kingdom, he wanted to be in the good books of the would-be king. But to his surprise, I was back from the dead and his plan failed. After the minister's confession, my image as a great warrior of Goryeo remained intact and he was executed by the public." The goblin answered.

"You remained in the power after minister was killed?" Seo Yoon wondered.

"Anniyo (No). If the people of Goryeo knew that I was resurrected, they would have started worshipping me like a god, which I never wanted. I lived in the dense woods for two hundred years and returned to the city only when people hardly recognised me. Over the years, I invested in various channels and earned a lot of money to keep living different identities to never let people know about my endless life. Sometimes I am Park Ji Yoon, Park Shin Yang or Park Ye Eun. I changed places, and lived various identities, but I never forgot a single death of people who served me over these years. I wished to die and be at peace, but I couldn't." The goblin uttered with tear-filled eyes.

"Your endless wandering life must be having a purpose. I am sure, once the purpose is fulfilled, you will meet the almighty." Jo Eun Sup said.

"The purpose of my life was to kill the mightiest evil spirit on this earth. I just killed the Black Soul and now the doors to the almighty are open for me." The goblin looked at the sky and smiled. "Ya Jeosung Saja (Heya! Grim Reaper), let's go back to Korea, I have to finish some work before we travel to the afterlife." He said to the grim reaper.

"Ne (Yes). The grim reaper nodded.

"Samchon (Uncle)" Seo Yoon looked at the goblin and wondered if she would really never be able to see him again. Her eyes reflected the innocence she carried since her childhood.

"Seo Yoona, it's time that you learn to live your life without the help of your uncle. Everything that I own in Korea is now yours. The house that we lived in, is still there for you." The goblin said keeping his hand on Seo Yoon's head.

"Anniyo (No). You can't leave me like this." Seo Yoon cried hugging the goblin.

"Will you do me a favour?" The goblin asked.

Seo Yoon nodded a yes.

"In the beginning of winter every year, I fly a lantern in the sky, for the king to whom I owe a debt in my heart for a very long time. Would you visit our house in winter and carry on this ritual for me?" The goblin asked.

"Ne (Yes)." Seo Yoon uttered nodding her head upside down.

The goblin looked at Rudra and signalled him to take care of Seo Yoon after he was gone. Rudra agreed, blinking his eyes.

"Wait." Jo Eun Sup shouted as soon as the goblin headed towards a huge pencil sketch hung on a tree.

"I have a question." Jo Eun Sup said.

"Why did the Black Soul kill your family?" The goblin spoke.

"Eo (Yes)." Jo Eun Sup confirmed.

"The little kid whom your father wanted to save was the first re-birth of king Wang Yi. The Black Soul possessed the kid to kill him and your father was making it difficult for her. That is why the Black Soul killed your family first." The goblin replied.

Listening to the goblin, Jo Eun Sup went numb.

"Your father was a great Shaman and you did justice to your family profession by learning Shamanism." The goblin patted Eun Sup's shoulder. "The police and a rescue team will be here any moment. It's time for us to leave." The goblin announced.

A blue and red flame appeared all around the pencil sketch. The goblin and the grim reaper waved goodbye to the humans and entered the sketch.

Thirty

04:45 IST

As soon as the goblin and the grim reaper disappeared, a team of police and medical rescue staff arrived at the trek. The police inspector quickly moved towards Dhruv's body and kept two of his fingers close to Dhruv's nostrils. "He is no more." The inspector announced taking off his hat. "How did it all happen? Are you guys injured?" He asked Rudra, Seo Yoon, and Eun Sup.

They all stood silent and kept sobbing hard looking at Dhruv's body. "Sir, I believe they all are in shock. Let's get their medical check-up done and we can start further inquiry once they are in a condition to tell us anything." The lady police staff suggested the inspector.

"Hmm." The inspector agreed. "Is there anyone else on the trek?" he asked.

Jo Eun Sup raised the index finger of his right hand towards the Kheerganga. Inspector guessed the fact that there must be someone else needing his help.

"Neha, you take them to Kasol safely, get their medical check-up done. I am trekking up with the team to check if there are more casualties." The inspector ordered.

"Sure, Sir." The lady police staff replied. "Please come." She signalled Rudra, Seo Yoon, and Jo Eun Sup to follow her down the trek.

18:00 IST

Shivi's body was retrieved by the police and the rescue team. A police case was filed to initiate a post-mortem of Dhruv's and Shivi's bodies. The post-mortem report clarified that the deaths happened due to an accident. The police case was then closed and the bodies were handed over to the respective families.

Rudra, Seo Yoon, and Jo Eun Sup were checked by the medical staff and there was no injury found on anyone's body. However, they took several hours to recover from the mental whirlpool of loss, regret, and haunting past.

Upon asking, they gave a statement that the death of Shivi and Dhruv was unnatural and it was all because of the Black Soul, which no one believed.

The police and the media stated that all the friends started trekking down during the night and due to lack of oxygen in the woods during the night time, they all suffered from hallucinations. Which in turn led to the accidental death of two of them.

Thirty One

16 November 2020, 18:00 KST (Seoul, South Korea)

Seo Yoon and Rudra stood on the porch of a huge palace-like building that was situated on the outskirts of Seoul. On their back was the building entrance and in the front was a huge lawn that was covered by snow all around. Despite the night being the darkest, the lawn was clearly visible courtesy of the bright lights in the building.

Seo Yoon held a white lantern in her hand. It had the name of the king Wang Yi scribbled over it. She lit the lantern and raised her hands to let it free in the open sky. While the cold winds took the lantern up in the sky, Seo Yoon turned to pick up another lantern. She took the colour brush and scribbled 'Park Jeong Su' over it.

"The second lantern is for your uncle?" Rudra uttered.

"Like my uncle used to fly a lantern for the king to whom he is indebted to, I have decided to fly a lantern for my uncle for whatever he did for me." Seo Yoon replied and lit the lantern.

She raised the lantern towards the sky to let the wind take its possession. As the lantern progressed toward the stars, tears of grief gushed out of Seo Yoon's eyes.

"Your uncle would keep turning back to watch you. He would be worried for you." Rudra hugged Seo Yoon and continued "That's why the ones left behind should live even harder." He wiped her tears.

"We might cry from time to time, but we should smile a lot and cheer up. Aren't you obligated to do that in return for the love you received from your uncle?" Rudra asked looking into Seo Yoon's eyes.

Seo Yoon nodded and looked at the lantern. "Sumchon (Uncle), be born to a good family and please live well in your next life." She uttered.

A blue flame appeared around the lantern and travelled to Seo Yoon's baby bump. She was due in two months. Rudra and Seo Yoon smiled looking at the baby bump and decided to name their kid 'Park Jeong Su'.